A LION'S PRIDE
THE SERIES

When A Lioness Pounces

A Lion's Pride, #6

Eve Langlais

Copyright © July 2016, Eve Langlais
Cover Art by Yocla Designs © February 2016
Content Edited by Devin Govaere
Edited by Amanda Pederick
Copy Edited by Brieanna Robertson

Produced in Canada

Published by Eve Langlais
1606 Main Street, PO Box 151
Stittsville, Ontario, Canada, K2S1A3
http://www.EveLanglais.com

ISBN-13: 978 1988 328 45 -4

Prologue

An ocean away, nestled within a lovely countryside, unmarred by progress, was a road, winding through a verdant forest that opened onto devastation.

Wide fields blazed, the tops of the crops bright torches, their smoke an acrid reminder of the land's bounty being squandered. Thatched roofs burned. People screamed and shouted as they scurried from their hovels, clutching their possessions and family.

Their homes weren't the only things on fire. The remnants of the castle burned merrily, the flames and smoke shooting high into the sky. The vivid green flicker, with a hint of purple, showed a fire born not just of wood and fabric, but of chemicals and potions, many of them quite rare, some irreplaceable. Their loss truly regrettable.

Fuck.

The expletive truly suited the mood, a dark and ugly mood. The enemy had struck at the heart of the empire. Destroyed decades of work, some of it inherited, and then fled.

How dare they leave before I can wreak retribution?

There was only one thing to do.

Cross the ocean in pursuit. Escape wasn't an option. Someone would pay…and just for the hell of it, so would anyone that got in the way.

Chapter One

The first time Gaston met her she didn't even look at him. Only the barest glance, an up and down flicker of her eyes then an abrupt dismissal.

Me. The most dangerous being in the room. Yet, she paid more mind to the club and his servants. Then again, she came with her so-called lion king as an enforcer, a lovely lush creature with her dark hair and bright eyes. Dressed quite dashingly too—all the ladies were, their black leggings hugging their every curve, enhancing the subtle nuances of their forms while their cropped tops only just covered their breasts, the peek of bared midriffs so distracting.

The perfect outfit for a fight. Gaston loved someone who came prepared and wasn't afraid. Things did devolve into violence. His servants, the whampyr he had created, had turned on him.

Unheard of. Especially for a master such as he who always treated his people right. Yet, many of his minions found their thoughts perverted. They chose mutiny. It had failed.

That was a few weeks ago, and since then, there had been more subtle attacks. Freezes on his accounts. Inspectors called to his place of business. Simple matters to deal with.

Until tonight. A new threat in the city had surfaced, a threat that involved him and, unfortunately, the lion king, Arik.

It made his lip curl to realize he was on a first-name basis with an animal. *When did that happen?* Since he'd moved into lion country and found a king who actively ruled it. Kind of refreshing to deal with someone almost intelligent for once. That didn't stop him from yanking the king's tail every chance he got.

Tonight, Gaston had come when Arik called because he couldn't ignore the threat in the subway system. Not when he knew of the monsters scuttling in the shadows. *They used to be my monsters.*

But his pets had gotten loose.

Arik, of course, didn't know they'd originally belonged to Gaston. Silly fellow, he ran into something too strange even for him and he'd known who to call. The High Council. And who had those old bastards called?

Only a few people could get Gaston to obey.

"I know the creatures he's talking about in the sewer are yours. You're the only one who makes them."

Because he was the only one with the correct spell. *"And?"*

"And you will make sure they locate them and get rid of them. We can't have the humans finding them."

Of course not, because then they would question, and questions meant discovery, and that meant tons of fun for those who liked to observe. It also meant sales on pitchforks and silver bullets.

Since he had more pressing concerns at the moment than hysterical humans, he behaved for now and did as asked. Gaston led the local lions to the sewers. It wasn't hard to follow the trail his pets had left.

Subways were fascinating places with so many shadowed nooks and crannies. Some of the tunnels led to platforms and hidden utility rooms, but there were also tunnels leading to nowhere. Dead ends that were perfect for a nest.

A nest he found. *"Illuminet."* The word of power whispered from him, and the marble-sized sphere in his hand lit and rose. The chamber lost its cloak of darkness. Round faces with large unblinking eyes peered as he hovered the ball of light overhead. The small bodies, dressed in their colorful scraps, huddled close together, looking so innocuous.

Standing beside Gaston, Arik wore a deep frown. "That can't be what's attacking folks. Look at them. They're shaking."

"With rage."

"They're barely a mouthful," Luna, another of Arik's lieutenants, observed.

"Appearances can be deceiving."

"Deceiving is right," Arik growled under his breath.

"They look like garden gnomes," someone observed.

As one the cherubic faces blinked, the tension in the cavern reached peak tautness.

"Now you've done it," Gaston muttered.

The rage of the *cabalus*—or what some more commonly called goblins—exploded. Tiny bodies expanded with berserker energy, stretching the rotund cabalus frames until they hulked at least six feet. Their flesh color turned a dark green and pimpled with warts and welts, each creature sporting a unique pattern. Some even had horns and tusks.

"Now that's more like it," a very feminine voice exclaimed with much excitement.

The one with the ugliest features—a sought-after distinction by the group—raised his arm and pointed at them as he gargled some noise. It led to much chest beating, and the wild eyes glowed with hunger. The cabalus had gone feral, reverting to their primitive ways instead of their more housebroken ones. A pity. They were great for patrolling the sewers by his home and place of business, until they'd just left one day. Like the mutiny of his whampyrs, their departure was out of character. The little creatures were ridiculously loyal if treated well. And he did treat his staff well.

Feral cabalus were pests that required extermination. He couldn't remember the last time it had happened.

The lion king and his forces did not flee when the goblinesque creatures attacked. On the contrary, most of them smiled, and one even shouted, "Hot damn, the big ugly one is mine."

He'd never seen such enthusiasm for battle. As for Reba, the woman who continued to ignore him, she was fascinating to watch. Frizzy hair, dark with hints of red, framed her face, her expression fierce. Her outfit proved perfect for fighting. How high her leg arched, the foot clad in stylish sneakers, her aim perfect and hitting Jodin—the cabalus who used to tend his roses—in the chin. He went down. He did not get back up.

His second-in-command, Jean Francois, stood by Gaston's side, watching the carnage. His servant chose to wear his human guise rather than his whampyr shape—for the uninformed that meant appearing as gray-skinned bats or gargoyles, depending on their transformation. No two whampyrs were ever alike except in one respect.

They were killers, and they thrived on blood. Unlike what some rumors stated, they were not vampires, although an element of their creation relied on that particular virus.

"I think we might have underestimated the strength of the animals," Gaston remarked, as the lions didn't even bother changing shapes to destroy the green nest.

"They only seem so strong because the inhabitants of this nest are addled. Look at how poorly they fight. I'm going to wager something infected them. The same thing that probably infected the others in the colony last month." The colony being the whampyrs that worked under Gaston.

"If there was an infection, then it didn't affect you," he observed, almost applauding as Reba slashed her nails down a rather jarring green face then smiled sweetly before grabbing its head, yanking it down, and ramming the hard top of her knee into it. *Crunch.*

"Whatever it was, it didn't affect those of us with half a brain. Although these two surprised me." Jean Francois looked over at Derrick and Leif, two more loyal minions that had survived his staff purge.

"Perhaps we should offer a hand to the animals?" Gaston itched to, especially when a rather large cabalus tried to snare the woman he couldn't stop watching.

I should step in and lend a hand.

Apparently, she didn't need his help. She squeaked, grabbed the goblin by the head, and heaved him over her shoulder, throwing him to the ground. Then she pounced. Her savagery took away his breath.

She is magnificent. And it irritated him that she didn't even seem to know he existed. And not for a lack of trying.

Jean Francois let out a low whistle. "Exactly what do you want to help them with? They are almost done."

With a wave of his hand, Gaston gestured to the bodies around him. "This requires cleanup before the human authorities arrive."

"A cleanup crew has already been called," Arik announced, the golden-haired lion king also looking rather pristine. While many cultures depicted the male as the defender and warrior, lions were different. With them, the females took the active role, hunting and protecting. A lion was a fierce thing, but also a bit lazy. He roused himself for only the big issues. Whereas the lionesses, they made small issues into big issues just for the hell of it. Or so Gaston had learned recently when he investigated them.

For example, he knew the local lion pride consisted of the alpha, Arik, who called himself king of the concrete jungle. Then there was Hayder, his beta, and Leo, his omega. Add to that Jeoff, who headed the security firm they employed to keep the lion pride safe.

But they didn't just have Jeoff, a werewolf with a small pack he used as enforcers. They had the lionesses, the fiercest force around. They took care of Gaston's renegade employees, and Gaston didn't even get a drop of blood on his suit. They resolved his situation and didn't demand payment.

But that didn't mean he shouldn't give thanks. At least to one person.

He stepped over the bodies and approached

the mocha-skinned beauty. She wore quite a bit of blood spatter. It didn't detract from her loveliness. Actually, she smelled kind of yummy, and before anyone wrinkled their nose, he would note he had an affinity for dead things.

"Miss Reba Fillips. I am Gaston Charlemagne. I don't think we've had the pleasure of truly meeting before." He offered her a short bow.

She bent over to fix a shoelace, and the front of her shirt gaped, wide enough that he could see her breasts in all their unfettered glory.

It was wrong to stare. That didn't stop him. So, of course, she caught him ogling.

She arched a brow. "Stare any longer and I'll have to charge you."

A real man didn't apologize for admiring a woman's assets, but he could commend her on other things. "I found myself most impressed by your fighting skill."

She flicked him a glance, head to toe. "I can't say that I'm very inspired by yours. I expected you to be more impressive." She dropped her gaze to a point below his belt buckle.

Feisty. Nice. He couldn't help but smile with plenty of teeth. "If I'd gotten involved, I might have ruined your fun like I did that night at the club." Apparently, putting everyone to sleep before violence erupted was considered the height of rudeness by the lions.

Her lips tilted. "Good point. You probably would have faced a few angry kitties if you'd pulled that sleeping stunt again. I do so enjoy a good workout."

No mistaking the innuendo. "I know of an

intense regime if you'd like to try it." He'd never been with a shifter before, mostly on account he thought there was something wrong with dating a pet, but he might have to revise that opinion. *She might be a cat, but she's definitely not tame.*

"The only thing I am into right now is a shower." Her nose wrinkled. "I smell like death."

"I know." Divine. "My place isn't far from here. You are more than welcome to the shower."

"My place is closer."

"Mine is *bigger.*" Yes, he might have purred those words.

And she...laughed. "You need to work on your pickup lines, sugar. That accent of yours might make lots of things sexy, but it can't mask cheesy."

Perhaps he'd gotten a little carried away. He didn't usually have to work very hard with women. He usually said hello. Sometimes, he just looked at a woman and they dropped their panties. Except for this woman. This woman just didn't seem that interested.

Perhaps he wasted his time. "Are you into guys?" he asked.

"Just because I didn't ask to ride your pogo stick doesn't mean I'm into girls. I like guys. I just don't like you."

He wanted to ask why not, but the soft cone of silence he'd woven around them to mask their conversation waned. And besides, he wouldn't beg.

At least he didn't mean to, but she presented a challenge. She intrigued him. He had to see her again.

If only she'd agree.

She ignored the flowers he sent telling her to call him. She ignored the text he sent asking her to dinner.

Unacceptable. She was an enigma that required unraveling. A challenge he had to conquer. So when Arik contacted him and said, "We've got more weird shit happening. We'd like you to take a look," he said sure, but he had one condition.

Chapter Two

"Where you going?" One of her best friends, Stacey, asked as Reba sauntered past the lobby on the main floor of the condo.

"The boss is making me go to the club."

"The horror." Her BFF clutched at her chest.

"Yes, the horror. It's on the other side of town, and it's not my style." Her style involved getting wasted in tottering distance of her apartment.

"Are you going to shake down the owner?" asked another of her besties, Joan's face now peering over the top of the divan.

"More like he wants to shake her down," snickered Melly, sprawled on one of the chairs. "Wasn't he the one sending you all that crap?"

"If he thinks he can buy me, he's going to learn differently." Really, flowers and chocolates. If he was truly serious about wooing, he'd have sent diamonds and designer shoes. A girl had to have standards.

"Later, biatches." She waved before she exited the building and got into the cab she'd called, still fuming.

I can't believe I have to go visit that pompous ass. But Arik roared, and Reba obeyed. That didn't mean she'd behave.

The stiletto tips of Reba's swanky heels clacked—a pair of Jimmy Choo's worth every penny

13

spent. *My precious shoes. Touch them and I'll rip your face off.*

The heels were made for her feet and gave her short stature a few extra inches. Not that she ever let her diminutive height dictate attitude. She owned plenty of attitude, along with confidence, her own car, and a healthy love of herself. That swagger meant Reba's ample hips swung, the loose fabric of her short skirt swishing as she strutted past the line waiting to get through the door for the club.

Lines were for sheep, and those who actually owned something called patience. Reba was pretty sure she'd traded her allotment of forbearance for a cookie when still a cub. As a result, patience was not one of her virtues, so screw waiting for her turn.

Ignoring the protests of those not graced with awesomeness, she placed herself ahead of them, only to find her entrance blocked by a wide dude wearing a black-collared golf shirt embroidered with the Club RainForest Menagerie logo; under it was stitched the word Staff.

"Stop."

Hello. Does he seriously think he can stand in my way?

Lacking a certain height advantage didn't mean shit to Reba. She peered upward and graced the bouncer with a look. *The look.* The kind that said, "Move your ass, bubba." In this case, bubba was a big ol' human, and he was silly enough to hold up a hand, blocking her path.

Oh hell no. He did not just do that.

He exacerbated his error. "You can't go in there."

The word can't was not one she recognized.

Mama had tried to teach her to know and respect limits. But her daddy always said can't was just a state of mind. Guess who she listened to? It wasn't for nothing Reba had a drawer at home dedicated to her Daddy's Girl T-shirts.

"I'm expected," she announced. More or less. And even if she wasn't, how dare he get in her way?

Don't hit him. Remember what Arik said about making sure anything I do is justified. Apparently, he'd agreed with Charlemagne to some sort of instigation rule. Which boiled down to, don't hit first. Even if tempted. Sad meow.

She behaved and tucked her hands behind her back, but that didn't stop the twitching of her hips, and she could practically feel a ghost version of her tail swishing behind her.

I can feel a rush coming on.

Don't let loose.

Bubba frowned down at her. "No one told me nothing about no special guests, so get to the back of the line."

Me? Stand in a line. Sorry, Arik, but she'd just been given all the reason in the world to get frisky. The human thought he could block her from entering. That kind of temerity deserved an answer.

Viper quick, she reached out, grabbed bubba's wrist, and yanked him close, close enough for him to see the primal amber of her beast glowing in her eyes. She showed a hint of fang too. "Don't get in my way. I've made bigger men cry." Always embarrassing when they sobbed for their mommies.

The big bouncer sneered.

She almost giggled in delighted. They just never listened. Such predictable fun.

A sharp twist of the hand and bubba hit the ground, his round face blanched in pain. She didn't break his wrist, but had to make a conscious effort. She did so forget her own strength sometimes when dealing with the sheep.

Arik said to not call them that.

Arik also said they shouldn't pounce on the pizza delivery boy until he squeaked. As if she and the crew listened. It was part of their Friday night ritual, along with daring each other to streak naked down the street. Although now, with their champion streaker Meena gone, and the cops waiting to ticket them for indecent exposure, they'd need to find a new triple lion dare for when the tequila bottle got low.

Still on his knees, bubba whimpered. Oops. She'd forgotten about him for a second there. Spotting the earpiece the bouncer wore, she leaned close and whispered, "Ready or not, here I come," before releasing the human.

He rocked back on his haunches and shot her a sullen glare, but he didn't try to stop her as she stepped inside. Smart man. She might have forgotten her manners if he tried anything.

See, boss, I held back. She'd stopped short of making him cry.

Past the threshold, she found herself in an outer chamber with benches lining the walls, their surface a dark color but painted with neon symbols and strange letters. Strange décor that she mostly ignored—although, she did make a note to send the club a business card. Whoever had designed and chosen the colors for this place should have flunked interior design school. This club needed help in a major way, but she wasn't here to sell her services—yet. That would be Monday's business.

Today she was here for the pride. She strutted to the door leading into the club proper. A pair of gaudily dressed females—more humans wearing bikini tops and tiny hip-hugging shorts better suited for a strip joint—gaped at her. They hugged clipboards to their chests, chests that surely felt inadequate next to Reba's own; all natural with cleavage made to swallow things whole, a great spot for storing her phone and spare cash.

The girls manning the door to the inner sanctum wore earpieces, and while the music made it impossible for Reba to hear, someone obviously said something given they gaped. *I think someone just told them who came to visit.* Kind of flattering, really, the way they ogled her rock-star style. Reba blew them a kiss and laughed as they recoiled.

What was it about her appearance that made them so leery of her? Had bubba whined about the mean lady? Did they bow before the greatness of her shoes?

Who cared? Actually, she did care because no one ever wanted to play. Apparently, Reba played rough. Luna wasn't the only one to break toys. "Ladies." She purred the word as she reached the second set of doors. The girls on either side recoiled.

A yank on the handle opened one side, and as she stepped through, she noted staff dressed in black T-shirts converging on her. Big dudes with big muscles.

Nice. At least they showed enough respect to send more than one. A lady liked to think she was appreciated. Before she could make them sing soprano, they halted, rather abruptly, and turned around, melting back into the shadows they used to hide. Probably because a certain stealthy guy stood behind her, not stealthy enough for her to not notice, though. His intriguing smell—the kind she wanted to roll in—gave him away.

"Couldn't you have waited a few more minutes? I was hoping for some exercise," she complained. Why did people always ruin her fun?

"If I'd known you were coming, I'd have had my staff lay out a path of rose petals and greeted you myself at the door," said a voice that belonged on late night radio—saying dirty things when she was alone in bed with her battery-operated friend.

As if she'd give Gaston Charlemagne, the mysterious new resident of their city, a warning? That wasn't how she operated. "Why waste time?" Reba announced. Arik had given her a job to do—*Find out what Charlemagne is doing in my city*—and instead of donating his flowers to the local old folks' home, or tossing the exotic chocolates he'd sent to the girls who dove off the couches to grab them, she took the direct approach and stalked him to his place of business. Club Rainforest Menagerie, emphasis on ménage. It seemed Mr. Charlemagne catered to those who preferred a more hedonistic lifestyle.

At least he used to. When he'd first opened shop, the club was only open to couples and single ladies. But since the incident with his staff going rogue, he'd transitioned to a more general club atmosphere. That meant no people making out in cages above the floor and better music for dancing.

Pivoting on her heel, she took in the svelte appearance of Gaston Charlemagne. Standing over six feet, he was impeccably dressed in black slacks, the front of them perfectly creased, a shirt of the deepest midnight blue, and a smile meant to wet panties. Good thing she didn't wear any.

He looks very yummy.

Smelled even better too.

Just like the first time Reba had met him, she had to wonder what the hell everyone was talking about when they said he had no scent. He smelled perfectly fine to her. More than fine. Decadent chocolate with a hint of smoky mystery. The aroma made her taste buds water.

Wanna take a bite.

"Go ahead." He bared his throat. "Have a nibble."

The invitation was less freaky than the fact that—*HE READ MY FUCKING MIND!*

Oh hell no. This was obviously the devil's work. Being a good Catholic girl—that was if owning the outfit with the short skirt and knee-high white socks counted—she knew what to do.

Fingers crossed, she held them in front of her as a ward. "Get out of my head, vile creature."

"Excuse me?"

"Be gone, oh stealer of souls. You shan't have my body or my blood." Okay, maybe he could have her body, but she was keeping her blood in her veins, thank you very much.

He arched a dark brow, dark as the hair on his head but missing the red highlights. "Exactly what insanity are you spouting? You do realize I'm not a vampire, right?"

So he claimed. As if a vampire would admit it. "I don't know what you are, but I do know there will

19

be no reading of my thoughts." Especially since said thoughts were veering in a direction that involved removing his clothes.

Pin him for a lick. A long, slow, raspy lick from those sensually curved lips down to the lollipop below the belt.

The thought might have started out as her inner kitty's, but the ending was all hers—and probably being read by him at this very moment! She shot him a glare and wagged her finger. "Ignore that last thought. I won't be doing that."

"Doing what?"

"What I was thinking." A thought she'd started having ever since she talked to him in the subway. She'd shot him down mostly because she didn't trust herself around him. Charlemagne had a very compelling quality about him. Even the other lionesses had noticed his allure.

They better not touch him.

His lips twitched. "And just what were you thinking, *chaton*?" he said with a purr her lioness envied.

"Don't pretend you don't know. I'm aware you can read minds." It said so in the vampire books she read.

At her accusation, rich laughter escaped him. "Hardly."

"Then how did you know I wanted to bite you?"

"Because you spoke your wish aloud."

She blinked. "I did?" Damn.

"But now I'm wishing you'd spoken aloud what you were thinking but a scant moment ago. What would a lady like you be thinking that would have her licking her lips and her temperature rising?"

"Lady." A snicker left her. Good thing he didn't know about the honey slicking her other set of lips. Then again, if he knew, maybe he'd do something about it.

Bad kitty. She was here on business, not pleasure.

"Did you get the flowers and gifts I sent?"

In other words, why did you ignore me? She smiled. "Nope." Utter lie and he knew it, but didn't call her out on it.

"I am surprised to see you here."

"Weird since you special requested me."

"But I didn't expect you to come. You're proven elusive thus far."

"It's called playing hard to get." She couldn't help but smirk.

He didn't let her keep the upper hand in their verbal sparring. "You finally succumbed, though. You *came*." The emphasis didn't escape her.

It sent a lovely shiver through her and made it hard to recall why she wasn't getting naked with the guy. He truly did get her motor humming.

Pounce him.

Pounce a guy who might be a vampire and lorded it over some bat dudes? Was she crazy?

Yes.

"I need a drink," she muttered. One that was four parts alcohol and zero parts juice. No point in letting filler get in the way.

"Allow me to serve you."

How did Charlemagne make that sound so dirty? Why did she enjoy it? No denying she rather savored his brand of bold style because she also had a tendency towards dauntless actions. Nothing scared her, not even this man, which was why she placed her hand on his forearm, only to find herself surprised. Since he'd abstained from the fight in the sewer, and even the one at his club, she'd assumed, rather mistakenly, that he was perhaps not a very physically fit man. The thick muscle hidden by his long sleeves said otherwise.

She squeezed. "I see someone works out."

"A man should always be ready in case he needs to indulge in strenuous activity."

"Stamina is important, but"—she cast him a look through partially shuttered lashes—"real skill doesn't need a whole lot of time."

Laughter barked from him. "True. But stamina can come in handy for other situations."

"I don't suppose those other situations involve loincloth mud wrestling with your staff." As they strolled through the club patrons, she found her gaze caught by a big fellow. Because she'd read the file, she knew his name. Jean Francois, supposedly Gaston's second-in-command and some kind of weird creature that was a cross between a bat dude and a gargoyle. What were they called? Wampers? Or was that wankers? She didn't know, hence why she was here to find out more. Especially find out more about the strange shit happening around town.

During the briefing, Arik and his close crew had talked about Gaston Charlemagne and his strange staff. What they knew so far—Charlemagne had moved into their city from overseas, and trouble soon followed. The man himself appeared to be some kind of supernatural. Just not a shifter. One theory said vampire. Totally cool. Another called him a mind-controlling alien here to implant them with foreign genetic code. Also kind of cool.

The man had so many secrets, and she wanted to find all of them out—even the ones hidden beneath his clothes. Some theorized he was the devil and had a tail. Reba had unofficially volunteered to find out.

Charlemagne wasn't the only one interesting the pride. His staff, their kind never seen before, was an enigma. They might shift into a hybrid bat-like creature, but they were nothing like the little nocturnal insect eaters, especially when you added in the fact that they drank blood.

Now, Reba wasn't averse to a little fresh snack. Her lioness wasn't a freaking rabbit subsisting on leaves and carrots. A hearty appetite required protein—and not just the male sausage variety. However, sucking blood from the vein of a human? Or a shifter? That set off her squick factor.

Don't eat things that talk. A lesson taught to all shifters at a very young age, especially the predator types. The avian groups still wouldn't let their kids attend the same schools, though. Make one joke about serving a swan up for Thanksgiving dinner and a whole race got offended.

But back to Charlemagne and his crew, a much smaller crew than he'd started with when he moved to the Pride-owned city. It seemed some of his *special* staff had gone on a kidnapping and killing spree, eating shifters belonging to the pride and other packs. A big no-no, and while those culprits were gone, the man who used to employ them remained, and Mr. Charlemagne seemed to think he was above their laws.

Snort. Yeah, no. Reba was here to set him

straight, get some answers, and maybe a few free drinks. Being a lioness, she would have fun while doing it—at his expense, of course.

"If the lady wishes to see my wrestling skills first-hand, then rest assured, I would be more than happy to show you. In person."

She cast the club owner a quick glance, and her lip curled into a partial smirk. "Sorry, but you're not my type." Her type usually roared. A pity they didn't stick around long after. Something about Reba scared them.

Pussies. Everyone knew Luna was the violent one and Reba was the lady.

Cough. Damned lioness had a hairball again.

"Ah yes, I should have guessed. You prefer malleable men who bow to your every command. You're right, we wouldn't be a good match since I like to give the orders." He gestured for her to go ahead of him up a flight of stairs, and as she passed, he slapped her ass and said in a husky murmur, "Especially in bed."

Me-fucking-ow. She couldn't have said what was hotter, his words, the slap, or the fact that skipping up the stairs, thus ensuring her skirt bounced and flared, meant he probably got a really nice view of her assets.

Look at that treasure and weep because these thighs won't be gripping you any time soon.

The mission came with a few rules from Arik—number one was don't start any fights. Number two was the same as number one. And number three was no sex with Charlemagne or his staff. Unless necessary—she added that last part since Arik surely forgot. Reba would take one for the team if needed.

Hell, I'd take it from him just because he's pretty to look at. Almost as cocky as a lion, she rather liked his forthright attitude.

The flight of steps took her to a small landing and a door. The guy guarding it, a fellow with no scent, stepped to one side, and she breezed through, already familiar from her briefing as to the layout of the club. She'd purposely avoided it since meeting him, all too aware of her insane attraction to the guy and determined to ignore it. Until the boss ordered her to come.

Now, since she didn't have a choice, she planned to make the most of it. Such a hardship, having to go clubbing for intel. The things she did for work. Sigh.

Giggle.

Despite his poor decorating choice, she would admit it was a swanky place. The main facilities for Club Rainforest were on the main floor—two dance floors, a few bar areas, a lounge with actual couches—covered in pleather for easy washing—and washrooms, a few unisex ones with big stalls that made hooking up easy. Or so she'd heard. Just because Reba abstained from partying here didn't mean the others in the pride did.

Only the DJ booth and the administrative offices were set higher than ground level.

All the better to watch over his business, I'll bet. And what did he see when he looked down? When the club catered to the more hedonistic side of humans, did he watch? Perhaps indulge in a little five-finger action?

She almost asked. Almost. He'd surely take it

as an invitation if she did, so she refrained as she shot him a glance from under almost shuttered lashes.

"Why do I get the impression you just had a dirty thought again?"

How did he read her so well? "Maybe because I did. A shame you couldn't read that one." She uttered a low chuckle as she turned away from him to truly take in the space.

A dim lamp standing in one corner provided the only illumination for the large room. A lack of proper lighting didn't impede her ability to see. Rather, it probably aided in seeing what happened down below. A wall of windows overlooked the busy club floor, and she stood close to it, peeking at the business Charlemagne had managed to build in a short amount of time. The change from almost pure sex club to dance didn't seem to have affected his attendance.

"Busy place tonight."

"It's busy every night, but my success as a business owner is not why you're here."

"You're right." She whirled. "I'm here to find out more about you." Every intimate detail, starting with his shoe size. A peek down showed decently-sized feet. As for his hands? Long but slender fingers, and he wore a ring on his left hand, not a wedding band, something thick and masculine with a thickset stone.

"So this is an interrogation?"

"In a sense."

"What if I choose to not tell you anything? What will you do?"

The intentional teasing dangled, and she

couldn't help but bat at it. "I guess I'll have to torture it out of you."

"That sounds promising." Again, he practically caressed her with his words.

It truly proved disconcerting, especially since she wanted his hands caressing her too. She distracted herself by sitting on the desk, crossing her legs, and canting her head. "Didn't you promise me a drink?"

"Promises are such powerful things and should never be taken lightly."

No they shouldn't because broken ones meant a lioness could wake up with her eyebrows shaved and a permanent marker mustache. Poor Stacey had spent weeks wearing a burka, but learned her lesson. Don't promise a girl sappy movies and ice cream and then blow her off for a man.

"Does this mean you lied about the drink?"

His lips twitched. "Any special requests?"

A glass of tall, dark, and handsome? *Behave.* "I'll take anything shaken, stirred, or even licked off my boob." She didn't need to grab and push them together. She wore the *good* bra today, the one that gave the finger to gravity. "Tequila is best done as a body shot."

"How about we stick to something a little more casual than hard liquor." He turned his back to her, and she spent the time he used pulling a bottle from a wine fridge—a man with class who drank from bottles and not boxes—to study him.

By the light suspended over the fridge, his hair glinted with hints of auburn, an odd hue for a man so obviously of European descent. That sexy accent of his gave his origin away. He kept his hair short, neatly trimmed enough that it didn't touch the collar of his button-down shirt. Wide shoulders led to a tapered waist and a trim ass. As Charlemagne turned, he caught her staring, and his dark brow arched. "Admiring the view?"

"Wondering what's hidden underneath." She held out her hand and let her fingers curl around the stem of the wineglass.

"I could strip to show you, but why ruin the mystery? You'll just have to leave wondering."

What arrogance, assuming she'd think of him. She couldn't help but laugh. "How cute, you're under the impression I care about you. Sorry, sugar, but you're so sadly mistaken." More lying. She had been thinking of him, but her momma had taught her to never let a man know.

"The thing is, *chaton*, I'm never wrong. You are intrigued by me."

"Because I have to be. You seem to think I'm here because I came of my own volition." She made a loud buzzer noise. "Wrong! I'm here because the boss sent me."

"Sent to ferret out my secrets by your so-called lion king."

The aspersion caused her back to straighten, and her eyes narrowed. "Arik *is* king of this city."

"Perhaps he's king of the cats, and even some of the dogs, but he has no sway over me. I am not one to be commanded. By anyone." He smiled, and it was a delicious kind of smile.

Cocky little bastard. But he'd have to try harder if he expected to impress her. Reba already knew some pretty arrogant men. "You say you won't be ordered around, and yet here you are, coming into our city on the sly. Setting up shop in secret."

"Secret?" Charlemagne laughed. "Hardly secret. You just never noticed what was right under your noses."

Because no one could smell Gaston but Reba, and no one could smell his men. How to detect a possible enemy in their midst if they couldn't rely on scent?

She swirled the contents of her glass and asked, "Who are you running from? Because successful business men don't up and leave and cross an ocean to start anew."

"Who says I'm running? Sometimes, a man gets bored and needs a new challenge."

She cast a glance over her shoulder. "And you consider getting people to dance and get wasted every night a challenge?"

"Running a club is more than just a room offering music and booze."

"Is that so? Then what makes yours so successful? Rumor has it your parties sometimes have a tendency of devolving into orgies."

He spread his hands, a gesture of innocence at odds with his wicked appearance. "I can't control what my patrons do. Sometimes, the mood strikes them and things happen."

"I know all about things happening, and I will add that hedonism isn't usually one of them unless encouraged by outside elements." Reba might own a wild side, but that side believed in a closed door when the clothes came off. But that closed door could be in public. The possibility of getting caught added a certain element of excitement.

"Are you accusing me of drugging my

clients?" Gaston crossed his arms.

"It's happened before. Or will you deny that glitter dust incident back during the troubles?" The troubles being shifters visiting the club kept disappearing, a snack for his employees. But that wasn't the only thing going on. There were a few reports of sparkly dust raining on the club attendees, a dust that dropped all inhibitions. Luna and Jeoff got caught in it when they were investigating. According to Luna, things got hot and heavy.

"The police ruled out foul play. A canister was found via one of the air intakes. None of the prints match the staff or patrons. The general consensus seems to be someone played a prank. It won't happen again."

She couldn't help but smirk as she said, "Is that your way of saying no orgasms tonight?"

Most guys would balk or get crude. However, Charlemagne wasn't a boy to gulp in terror at her boldness. This wasn't an unruly male who tried to jump her body with no finesse. This was a man, in his prime, oozing confidence.

His eyes flashed with a possible crimson light, or was it the strobing beams inside the club that gave that impression? His lip turned up at only one corner, a sexy hint of humor. "Who said there would be no orgasms?"

"Me, because, unfortunately, the boss said no touching. I'm just supposed to get you to spill your guts." Figuratively, not grossly.

"I wouldn't have to touch you to make you come." He took a seat across from her, giving her the height advantage. He sat very much at ease, his legs slightly spread, elbows on the armrests and his fingers laced. "I could make you cream yourself from here and never lay a finger on you."

Did he think he could sweet-talk her into coming? Her nose wrinkled. "Gotta say, sugar, I never was big on the whole dirty-talk thing. Personally, I think if you have enough breath to speak then you're not using enough tongue."

His lips definitely twitched that time. "My technique doesn't need words. I would just make you come."

Perhaps he could. That velvety voice of his acted like a caress, and excitement hummed inside her. Heat pulsed, too, and not a heat born of alcohol from the wine. "Is this where I'm supposed to be overcome by your slick innuendos, pounce on your lap, and swoon at your expert technique?"

"Pounce if you like."

"I don't like."

"And you lie again. Just for that, I won't make you come until you ask me."

"I'll never ask you." Asking was for desperate girls. Reba just expected seduction to happen.

He shook his head, the reddish hints flashing. "By using the word never, you've made sure it will happen. There are forces out there, evil forces, that will work against you." He uttered it so seriously she couldn't help but giggle.

"I can't believe you're superstitious."

"Call me old-fashioned."

"An old-fashioned man doesn't wait for a woman to beg. He takes."

"When it comes to sex, I'm a modern male. I think I shall enjoy it when you ask me to pleasure you. In the meantime, while you fight your natural urge, tell me, what else did you want to know about me?"

Was he as good as he claimed? Only one way to find out.

Down, kitty. There will be no show and tell. Because she wouldn't ask him to make her come— even if she was a tad curious. Instead, Reba went with the question everyone wanted an answer to. "What are you?"

"Nothing you've ever encountered before."

"Well, duh. But what is that?"

"A secret for now." He cocked his head. "Next question."

She let him skip the what he was for now. "Why are you here?"

"Just pursuing business opportunities."

"But why here specifically?" she prodded.

His dark eyes caught her gaze. "Perhaps fate brought me here for a reason. Perhaps there is something in this city that I need. Something that I must have in order to survive."

She snapped her fingers. "You came for the food, didn't you? Because you know we do have the best steak house in town. Often overlooked are their side dishes, though. The roasted potatoes are to die for. Literally, like don't touch mine, or I will stab you with a fork."

"I'll try to restrain myself," spoken by Charlemagne so dryly.

"So we've got a date?"

"What?"

"Date. Are you slow or something? You just said you promised to not eat my food, which implies we're going on a date. Lucky you, I'm free tomorrow night to meet you at the Lion's Pride Steak House. Be sure to look pretty." She patted his cheek and hopped off the desk. "Is five o'clock too early? I hear it's supposed to be a bright sunny day tomorrow."

"Five o'clock is fine."

"See you then." She blew him a kiss and swished to the door, only to squeal as a hand swatted her ass. "Sugar!" she squealed, amazed at how quickly he moved.

"What is it, *chaton*?"

He didn't sound close enough, and when she whirled to look, he still sat in his chair. Nowhere near her butt. Spooky.

"Did you touch me?"

"Would you like me to?" he countered.

Yes. She could feel the rush under her skin, her ghostly tail flicking, every part of her urging her to go with her instincts. And those instincts wanted to pounce. But then he'd win and the game would be over. Where was the fun in that? She liked to play.

"I'm not going to make it that easy for you. If you want this"—she indicated her figure—"then you'll have to work for it. Now remember what I said about looking pretty. I want you to look good in case any of my crew is there." *Who am I kidding? They'll all be there because I'm going to call them and tell them to go.* "Don't be late, or I will *start* without you," she sassed.

"I'm fine with you getting things ready for me. Wear a dress," was his comeback just before the door behind her slid shut.

Oh she'd wear a dress all right, with no panties. *We'll see who does the begging tomorrow night.*

Meow!

Chapter Three

A date. Gaston was going on a fucking date. How the fuck did that happen?

When Arik had contacted him demanding meetings, he'd blown him off. Gaston didn't answer to household pets. He didn't consort with them either, and yet, he began revising that particular rule when the mocha beauty with the sassy attitude wouldn't leave his mind. How could his brief meetings with Reba leave such a lasting effect? He wanted to see her again, now. Yet, in this modern time and place, he couldn't just pluck her off the street. Nowadays, they called it kidnapping and forced confinement. Back in the day, it was considered part of the courtship.

So he'd negotiated with Arik to work exclusively with Reba. He'd meant only to talk to her, needing to figure out why she kept featuring so prominently in his dreams of late. He'd tried to be more modern, sending flowers and gifts. She didn't reply. Despite his best efforts, she ignored him.

Ignored me. The indignity of it still burned.

And he couldn't throw her into chains for her temerity, or withhold her saucer of cream—*I'd rather give her my cream*—so he negotiated with the lion king and used her loyalty to her pride to have her sent to him.

He'd thought himself prepared to handle her.

He was a man of suave replies and cool responses. With everyone but her it seemed. He might have managed to not spill any secrets, but somehow, he was going on a date with Reba. Reba with the sexy curves. Reba with the wild hair that wanted tugging. Reba with the smirking smile and outrageous mouth made for sucking.

Instant boner.

Fuck. The woman might have left his presence, but her essence lingered, a distraction he could ill afford. Not with events beginning to spiral.

The door slid open and his second-in-command, Jean Francois, entered.

"I see the alley cat is gone. What did she want? Was she sent to spy?"

"She is but a harmless stray. Nothing to worry about. Care to have a drink with me?" He tilted his empty glass before standing and arranging to refill it.

"How about instead of a drink, I give you a shot to the head? What are you thinking meeting with one of the pride cats? I thought the plan was to avoid them after the subway incident."

"Even I cannot refuse a command from the High Council." Those who did never lived long enough to regret it.

"They told you to work with the felines, not invite the one you're lusting after to meet with you privately. What makes you think she won't run back to her king and claim you made unwanted advances?"

"She wants me to seduce her. She just won't admit it."

"You're playing with fire."

"No, I'm playing with her because she pleases

me. It's been a while since I've been with a woman." A long while. None ever engaged him past the physical relief. None inspired him to make ultimatums.

"If you're horny, then hire an escort." A suggestion by his ever-practical second-in-command.

But an escort wasn't Reba, a woman who took down his biggest bouncer with ease. A woman who didn't say what she should. She was utterly fascinating. And dangerous. So dangerous for his health.

She'd probably kill me if she knew what I was.

The possibility of death served only to add an extra layer of flavor to his attraction.

Thick fingers snapped in front of him. "Pay attention. What the fuck is wrong with you? We don't have time for you to be distracted by a broad."

No time, and yet, he couldn't help himself. He forced her from his thoughts. "She's interesting." Nothing more. He couldn't allow her to get close, not with his unresolved business. "Her alpha sent her to ferret out information."

"And did she get any?"

Gaston rolled his eyes. "What do you think?"

"I think that you've been itching to see her again since you met her. And tonight, you proved it by sniffing after her skirts the moment she got here."

Not entirely his fault. The skirt barely covered a luscious frame, and it didn't help that he now knew she didn't believe in underpants. How easy it would have been to slide a hand under the skirt and stroke those velvety folds.

"Snap the fuck out of it," JF barked. "We've got important shit to discuss, and I can't do it while you're mooning."

"I don't moon." Although he might masturbate tonight for the first time in a while.

"Whatever. Anyhow, I came to find you because we found another one of those canisters by the roof vent. We disarmed it before it hit the ventilation system." Another attempt to spread Surrexerunt Ludere, a fancy name for the orgy dust that someone kept attempting to dump on his patrons. More of an annoyance than a threat. It served as a message that his enemy had noticed him. About time. This was the eighth city he'd chosen to set up in since his arrival from overseas. "How are the canisters being planted without us noticing?" No one ever saw them being carried in and positioned. The cameras by the airshafts always went fuzzy before they appeared.

"I don't know the how, but whatever it is screws with the signal for the cameras."

"It seems like the work of our enemy."

JF shrugged. "Possibly, or maybe one of the fuckers that mutinied left instructions and stuff before dying and someone is just finishing the job."

"A shame I can't kill them again," he muttered. Gaston didn't show leniency to those who betrayed him. "They were weak and let their baser natures overtake common sense." A flaw of the whampyrs.

"They might have been easily swayed, but now that they are gone, we are short of soldiers." With no way of easily making new ones. Each whampyr took a certain set of circumstances to create. Yes, create, and Gaston still cursed the fact that he'd lost so many of them in an uprising that should have never happened. Usually, soldiers were faithful to their master.

But something went wrong. Something had corrupted their base desire to serve. He'd yet to find out what, although he suspected. Until he could close that loophole in their loyalty, it could happen again. He hoped not. He rather liked JF, and he'd hate to have to kill him. He would, though. Gaston wasn't one for sentimentalities when it came to his own wellbeing.

"Now that you're done chastising, do you have anything else you wanted to say?" Gaston asked. He encouraged honesty with JF, but didn't always like it.

"Stop obsessing over the girl."

"I can't." Especially since he had a date to go on in less than twenty-four hours.

I won't go. A resolve that didn't work.

Next thing he knew, the hours skipped past and he was three minutes early the next day at the restaurant, impeccably dressed and calling himself an idiot for going. He regretted it the moment he walked into the restaurant.

First off, the hostess who greeted him recognized him. Her eyes widened. "Holy corn niblets on a cross, you came. She wasn't fibbing." The hostess snickered. "Wait until the ladies get a load of you." Then she grinned. Grinned the whole time she personally took him to his table, his two-seat table in the middle of the large dining room, a dining room mostly comprised of shifters and the humans that knew of them. And, no, he didn't do anything so primitive as smell the air to decipher this. Anyone could tell, just by their look. The look of an animal barely contained in civilized skin.

It never failed to amaze him that the humans never noticed the wild animals in their midst. Then again, neither human nor shifter ever recognized Gaston for what he was until too late.

The patrons of the restaurant stared, not even making a pretense of hiding their interest. He ignored them, because he really didn't give a fuck. He sat and played *Stickman Golf* on his phone until someone sat across from him. He flicked a glance over, noted it was not Reba, and returned to his game.

A throat cleared.

Whack. His pixel ball missed.

"I said ahem," followed by a bigger throat clear.

Why did some people not get the hint to leave him alone? He raised his gaze. "Can I help you? Perhaps offer you a lozenge or a more permanent solution to your breathing problem that involves removing your head?"

A redhead, her hair swept up with clips, her eyes ringed in dark liner, eyed him. She didn't balk at his threat. "I'd like to see you try."

"That would require more effort than you're worth." He went back to his game, pleased to note that, thus far, his interest in a certain feline was specific to Reba. This woman and the others in the room did nothing to rouse his intrigue or other body parts.

"So I guess you're that dude."

"What dude is that?"

"The dude with that club."

"Yes." He went back to putting and sinking his pixel ball.

"We've met before. At that monster bash when Luna was being held prisoner and in the sewers."

"Perhaps. I don't recall." He did know her from his files, though—Stacey, event coordinator for the pride—wedding, birthday, anniversary, guerilla attack. She made sure events went off without a hitch.

"Why are you here?" she asked, more pesky than a fly.

"This is a restaurant, correct?"

She nodded.

"Then it stands to reason I am here to have a meal." The smells coming from the other tables and the kitchen seemed to indicate a certain degree of competence.

"You're eating here by yourself?" she fished.

He nibbled at her line. "I am expecting a companion."

"You mean a date? Here?" She blinked and turned her head. She didn't say a word, and yet, another woman slunk close and noisily dragged a chair over to the table. "He's waiting for his date," she informed the newcomer.

"Here?" They both stared at him.

Since it bored him, he continued to play golf.

"He eats? Wouldn't it be more like drink?" asked the blonde with short hair. Joan, the athletic instructor for the pride. She ran a seriously tough boot camp according to gossip.

"I'll bet he's into that tartan meat."

"I think you mean steak tartare." He couldn't help but correct, and he made the mistake of raising his gaze, to realize they stared at him, three felines now, seeing as how another of the women had joined them, draping herself on the lap of the first.

The unblinking nature of their appraisal didn't stop him from returning to his game, but he flubbed his shot.

"So, are you a vampire?" one of them boldly asked.

The obsession persevered. He sighed and addressed the multiplying felines across from him, four now by his count. "No I am not a vampire, and the lady opening the shades and letting in the sunlight is only bothering those in its direct beams. I have a place on a beach in Punta Cana where I spend time tanning. I also swim in the ocean during the daytime. Is that answer enough?"

The fifth woman to join the pile around him asked, "Do you swim with trunks or in the nude?"

"You'll see when I Snapchat the pics on our vacation." At Reba's arrival, the stares moved from him to Reba—who looked decadent in her light blue shirtwaist dress. Buttons down the front begged to be popped, except there was a bit of an audience.

"You're his date?" the redhead asked. "I thought you weren't interested."

"I'm not."

"Can I have him? He's interesting." A green gaze stripped him naked.

"No, you may not have him. He's mine at the moment." Reba tossed her head, the regal lift showing off the dangling hoops hanging from her lobes. "He asked me out, so be jealous elsewhere. Scat." Reba swept her hands, and suddenly, Gaston was back to no uninvited guests and a bemused expression surely since she'd called him *mine*.

"You're late," he observed. He was a man who liked punctuality.

"I'm here. You're welcome."

"You are the one who set the time and place."

"I know. And you came." She smiled at him, the sharp-toothed grin of a predator closing. "And you look very pretty, sugar."

How could she tell since most of his outfit was hidden by the table? Then it occurred to him he still sat. How utterly rude for a man raised with old-fashioned values. He jumped to his feet, his manners seeing him gripping the chair across from his and holding it out for Reba. "Won't you join me?"

She actually looked surprised, and was it him, or did he hear an "Oooooh" from more than one voice? He also heard a slap and a hissed, "How come you don't do that for me?"

Reba seated herself, and he resumed his own spot. He waited until the waiter appeared to fill her glass with wine before raising his and clinking it to hers. "To getting to know each other."

"With clothes. And"—wink—"without."

Their conversation didn't go unnoticed as someone hollered, "Don't forget to check him for a tail when you get him to strip."

He didn't sputter his wine, but it was close. "A tail?"

She waved a hand, utter negligence at its finest. "Some of the wagers going around claim that you're the devil. But I've seen your ass. It's too fine to be hiding a tail."

"Thank you, I think."

"Thank me later when I've groped it to be sure."

He needed a big sip after that. His dinner companion seemed determined to keep him off balance. "I didn't think you'd come," he said after swallowing the fine vintage. The research he'd done showed lionesses, especially those raised in a strong pride, tended to play games. Especially power games. Just look at her showing up without warning the night before, trying to take him off guard.

It had worked.

And now look, he still danced to her tune. It was rather humbling for a man of experience like himself to be so addled by a woman.

"Not come? I'm all about coming." She grinned and leaned forward, the neckline of her dress gaping and showing her breasts, once again not constrained by the modern version of a brassiere. Awful things keeping breasts prisoner. *The only things that should cup her breasts are my hands. And maybe my mouth.* He possessed an especially intense desire to slide his cock between them.

The very idea was almost enough to make a man drool—if he were an animal. Gaston took another sip of his wine. At this rate, he might need a few bottles. "Is this your coy way of asking me to please you? It's a little public, but that's your choice."

"If I ask, you'll know. But I won't. I'm not a slut who throws herself at a man."

"A shame." Really it was, especially since he would have totally respected her after, and even paid for the cab ride home.

"Yes, it is a shame. I have to admit being disappointed. I thought you were a man of action. A guy who takes charge."

"Getting you to ask for me to pleasure you is

all about me taking charge." He fixed her with an intent gaze. "And you will ask." Because no way would he beg.

"Not likely. And just to be sure, I took care of business before coming out."

The revelation caused an instant visual of her with her hands between her thighs, busy stroking, her lips parted, her skin flushed... He couldn't stop an instant erection. And she knew it, too, the little hellcat.

Her lips curved. "Maybe next time I'll send you a Snapchat as I'm doing it."

He almost shouted yes. Then he found his balls. "If I wanted to look at porn, I'd browse the Internet. I'm a man who prefers in-the-flesh encounters. And there are plenty of those around." He purposely looked at the redhead, and when she smiled back, he winked.

The wine splashing his face took him by surprise.

"Oops. I don't know how my hand slipped. Let me get you something for that." Reba snapped her fingers, and the waiter, trying hard not to smirk, approached with a towel.

He stood. "Don't bother. I have this." Gaston did a snap of his own, and the moisture left his skin, wrung back into the glass it had left. As Reba gaped, Gaston ducked down and whispered, "Jealousy becomes you. Call me when you're ready to beg me." Then he straightened and shook his phone at her. "Sorry, but business is calling. Eat whatever you like. I've already prepaid for your meal and that of my new lady friends."

With a wink, he did his second trick of the

night. One minute he stood there in plain sight, and the next he disappeared, a simple trick of the light that he'd mastered a long while ago. It didn't fool Reba.

"Nice try, sugar. I know you're there. I still smell chocolate."

He smelled like chocolate? How very strange. Something to ponder about later. He dropped a light kiss on Reba's neck and felt her shiver. He wanted to do more, but refrained, instead whispering, "Until next time, *chaton.*" Before he could change his mind, he exited amidst squeals of "How did he do that?"

The more real question was, how did she do that? How did she manage to twist him until he wanted to drop on his knees to beg? He left before he forfeited the game and seduced her.

Funny how the throbbing ache between his legs didn't feel like he'd won.

Chapter Four

With a disappearing act to rival a magician in Vegas, Charlemagne left Reba with wet girly parts and an excited crew.

Stacey arrived at her table first with a, "Holy fuck, biatch, what the hell was that?"

Only like the hottest thing ever.

"Please tell me the body hiding inside that suit is as hot as he is," exclaimed Joan, the fitness buff of the group.

How about hotter?

"I think someone is tongue-tied," sang Melly.

The group around her grew as the girls all tried to make sense of her short date with Charlemagne. Short, and yet, she'd never been on such an intense one. The man left her wanting more, and despite her claim, Reba already knew her battery-operated friend wouldn't do the trick tonight. Gaston left her needing. Wet. Aching.

A part of her wanted to hunt him down, pounce his ass, and do something about the fire he'd started.

He could start by dousing the heat with his tongue. But then she'd lose the game, a game that had just begun. She needed to slow down if she wanted to win. She also needed a way to cool her ardor. A dip in the river would ruin her hair, but a trip to a crime scene might just do the trick.

"We need to go visit a graveyard." Luna's arrival and announcement managed to trump the excitement over the Rainforest club owner's brief appearance.

"Why are we visiting a graveyard at night?" Reba asked. And, more importantly, was she wearing the right clothes?

"We are going because we got a call about shit happening."

Their resident geek, Melly—who religiously watched every *Walking Dead* episode—hopped up and clapped her hands excitedly. "OHMYGODTHEZOMBIEAPOCALYPSEISHE RE. I'm ready for you, Daryl." She ran out of the restaurant shrieking in excitement, probably off to get dressed in her zombie fighting gear.

The rest of the lionesses just shrugged and closed ranks. "What's happening in the graveyard?"

"Someone's been playing robber in it. There are some empty graves. Three of them now, plus two more missing bodies slated for the furnace."

"Missing bodies?" Stacey grinned as she looked around at the faces. "You know what this means."

"This sounds like a mission for the—"

"Baddest Biatches!" The scream saw them tossing hands over the middle of the table, and a lot of slapping occurred, most of it intentionally painful. Welcome to the lioness club, where their bond was tight, if violent, and they thought nothing of piling into a few vehicles and visiting the home of the dead after dark. They even kept such things like flashlights and rope and dark skullcaps in the trunk. It made traffic stops with searches interesting to say the least.

Being prepared meant a few of the girls entered the graveyard carrying shovels on their shoulders. A biatch never knew if she'd need to smash in a few zombie skulls or bury some bodies. Best friends never asked questions; they just dug the hole.

Personally, after conducting many tests—on melons, the skull not gourd kind—Reba had discovered the baseball bat was her most effective choice in fighting the undead. Made of lightweight aluminum, the hilt wrapped in bright pink hockey tape, and the length of it bedazzled—because a girl could never have too much glitter—she loved how the thing never failed her, saved her expensive nails, and matched almost all her outfits, like her current one of track pants, T-shirt and a hoodie. She'd changed out of her dinner dress, the lack of underwear not exactly conducive to graveyard traipsing. Good thing she'd also changed out of the stilettos she'd worn for dinner. Reba's flat tennis shoes didn't sink in the soft soil, and even if they got mucky, she wouldn't cry because they didn't cost her a month's rent.

Keeping pace with Luna, Reba grilled her bestie for some more information on the situation. The ride over involved the radio blasting as they played car karaoke, making it hard to get any details. "So what's the cops' theory on the missing bodies?"

"The fuzz don't know yet, and we're going to keep it quiet for the moment," Luna stated.

"It might be kind of hard to hide the fact there are bodies missing." Relatives tended to get upset about that kind of thing. No, she wouldn't tell how she knew that particular fact. The settlement had a gag order on it.

"Actually, no one needs to ever know because whoever took the bodies left the coffins behind, and they were buried empty."

Reba stopped walking, and so did Luna, letting the others get ahead. "Then how did anyone know they were missing?"

"By fluke. Apparently, some guy whose girlfriend died in a freak accident decided to pull a Mary Jane's last dance and broke into the funeral home the night before the burial. He then lost his shit because her coffin was empty and he thought she was a zombie who was going to come after him for brains."

"Was she?"

Luna shrugged. "Don't know. Haven't found her yet, and he's been sedated and put under watch for seventy hours."

"So that's one body missing. What about the others?"

"The funeral director got a little suspicious, so he went looking. Turns out another body scheduled for cremation yesterday went missing from its box too. So…we went digging."

"Who is we?"

"Me and Bernie."

"Bernie being?"

"The dude that works here. Anyhow, Bernie called me on account I'm the liaison for weird shit in the city—"

"Since when?"

"Since always, just like you're the one we call when we need some answers."

"How come I don't have a cool title like

liaison?"

"You're the answer chief."

"I like liaison better."

Luna glared.

Reba smiled.

"I think I'm starting to really understand Jeoff's point of view. We are difficult to deal with."

"The most impossible."

A grin split Luna's lips. "No wonder we're awesome."

Indeed. So awesome they were in a cemetery skulking around before the cops got wind, which the funeral home was not keen on happening. Missing bodies wasn't good business or news for anyone.

"What should we be looking for?" Luna asked as various lionesses split off on the paths, going in different directions to cover more ground.

"Something. Anything. We'll let the other girls cover the grounds and check out the fresher burials. You and I will hit the funeral home itself and see if we can figure out who took the bodies."

Except, hours later, at the butt-crack of dawn, dirty—because dust bunnies lurked even in morgues—sweaty—because that damned incinerator room was hot—and empty-handed—because Luna wouldn't let her keep the amputated one she found in the fridge—they had to concede defeat. Despite going over every inch of this place, they found not a trace of evidence. Not even a scent. Nothing left behind as a clue. It was too clean.

Which, in itself, could mean only one thing in Reba's mind. She knew of only one group of beings that didn't leave a scent. Lucky her, their boss didn't live far, and he still owed her a dinner date.

Looks like he'll be dining in.
Meow.

Chapter Five

Upon leaving Reba, Gaston went straight to his appointment. He actually didn't lie about having business. The text message had arrived in the nick of time before he could do something foolish, such as seduce Reba as she demanded.

As if a mere woman is going to order me around. The very temerity of it made him steadfast—and adrenalized. A part of him understood they both played a game of dominance, and only one of them could win. *One of us will have to give in.* Would that be so bad? In the end, win or lose, it didn't matter since it would result in pleasure.

Decadent, hot, and naked pleasure...

It almost proved enough to shred his patience, but he had maturity on his side. No point in rushing the dance. A bit of restraint meant seeing the end of the race. Drawing out the anticipation would make the victory all the sweeter.

Walking away from Reba was its own form of foreplay. He'd enjoyed the feel of her shock when he slipped out of sight, her gasp as he touched her. Despite his cloaking, he could have sworn he felt her watching him leave. Being a man, he didn't turn around to see if she truly did.

One thing did surprise him. He expected her to come after him. Reba wasn't one to tolerate a man walking away from her.

Unless she didn't care.

Surely he didn't suffer from disappointment that she hadn't followed. It was good she stayed behind. Gaston didn't want her to follow or get involved in his business. Not when the latest news from JF indicated it would probably soon turn deadly. The tiny games played thus far were coming to an end, at least according to the short and yet quite serious text he received.

Rumor has it the dead walk in this town. There was only one thing that could allude to. The enemy was here, had noticed him, and now began to move against him.

Gaston slipped into his car a few blocks from the restaurant and entered his club less than twenty minutes later. He met JF in the upstairs office.

"Where were you?" his second asked.

"Having dinner."

"With who?" JF crossed his big arms over his chest. "And keep in mind, you reek of pussy."

And JF smelled like Mongolian beef. It made Gaston hungry for the dinner he skipped. "I thought pussy was a good thing?" he remarked with a leer.

"Not when it brings trouble."

"They always bring trouble." But, sometimes, a man welcomed it. *I could use a little spice in my life.* "If you must know, I had a dinner date."

"With her?"

"I don't think that's any of your business."

"Anything that affects you is my business. Especially when you're playing with the local wildlife. What happened to not fucking with pets?"

"Perhaps that was spoken in haste." A long time ago, those who could swap skin for fur had been a rarity and usually kept in captivity. It led to some very feral shifters, men and women who weren't much better than animals.

Then that Moreau fellow began playing God, and whole new breeds emerged. Smarter creations who, one day, got loose. In the beginning, they were few in number and spent time hiding, hidden from everyone. They flourished, their numbers multiplying. They formed packs and prides and sleuths, banding together for strength. Thinking themselves equals.

What a concept. But then again, having now spent some time with the shifters, he could grudgingly admit they were more intelligent and likeable than expected.

So likeable I want to see a certain feline again.

"Be careful. You can't trust them. Can't trust any woman."

His second had betrayal issues, so instead of expounding on the virtues of the female form, Gaston veered their conversation to the real reason for their meeting.

"Your text implied the dead are walking. What have you heard?" He poured himself a drink as JF sat at the desk and angled the large computer monitor so Gaston could also see.

JF pointed a thick finger at the mini windows layered on the screen. "Some of the reports are incomplete. We haven't fully penetrated the agencies for this city, we're too short on men for that, but a few snitches have come through. The funeral home robberies have begun."

"Don't tell me we found the right place for once in the early stages?" Locating the enemy before they dug in proved a daunting task. All the computers and hackers in the world didn't mean shit if there was no trace to be found.

The enemy knew how to hide.

But I'll find you. I always do, and then I'll crush you again.

"I don't know if we're early. Ten years is a long time. Surely there would be more progress if this was the base city, which was why I began searching the outer boroughs."

A city they'd chosen at random when the last one proved a bust. When it became clear it was time to move on, he jabbed his finger at a map, and they'd relocated once again. How many places now? His European home seemed so far away now and foreign. He'd not visited in over a year. His stint in the United States had changed him. The fast pace and vivid nature of the population drew him. But more and more, he felt as if he searched for something, something that had nothing to do with revenge.

Was that what attracted him to Reba, the brightness of her spirit? The fact she *lived*?

His fingers tapped the armrest of his seat. "Since you're mentioning the boroughs, I am going to assume you found something."

"A few items of interest. Mentions of bodies going missing in morgues. Some grave robbing. The police have yet to link all the incidents together."

"I'm sure they've been encouraged to look the other way." In some respects, the enemy tactics never changed. "Any theories on a stronghold location?"

"Not yet. The incidents thus far haven't

shown any pattern. We'll keep digging."

"Dig fast." Because now that the enemy had noticed Gaston's presence, things would truly heat up. *And me without any serious forces.* Losing his whampyr army was a blow, as was losing his household goblins. But when push came to shove, Gaston was his own most powerful weapon.

And knowing that was why he slept so well at night.

*

Blue skies darkened as smoke smothered the land in a smoggy veil. A billowing black cloud never meant good things. He saw it as an ominous harbinger of doom. No matter how fast he moved, how much he wanted to be there, he arrived to find only a smoldering ruin.

Gone, all gone. All he'd loved. All he owned. The last memories of his family. Burned to a crisp. Not enough to be betrayed, now he was without a home and his treasures. The rage of loss dropped him to his knees in the ashes, the fine silt of it lifting to coat him in the remains of his life. The coals buried deep within the ash heated his flesh, charring his clothes. Who cared if he burned with them? How could he survive alone?

The loneliness within threatened to tear him apart.

I did survive. I moved past this low point. Moved past because he gave himself a new purpose. A reason to rise each morning.

Vengeance.

Vengeance meant he didn't give up.

Vengeance helped soothe the pain of losing everything. Especially his sister. However, sometimes his haunted dreams forced him to recall the past. *It's but a nightmare, and I can control what happens.*

The knowledge let him move past the smoldering ruins, floating ghostlike away from the swirling ashes, only to find himself slammed into a different reality. A more recent and familiar one.

He stood at the entrance to his club, a gaudy place by day, a decadent ballroom of pulsing sound and bodies at night. He never tired of absorbing the bright energy that was life. A man accustomed to death, he enjoyed the vibrancy of people getting together and allowing themselves to just relax and float free.

That living energy was absent in his dreams, as the floor gaped wide and empty of patrons. Silence reigned, the usual hard-pulsed music absent. Shadows covered most of the space, hidden corners and nooks revealed in sporadic bursts by the always-moving strobe lights. The various gem-hued beams danced around, each revelation a breath-held moment, waiting for something to appear.

Will it have claws? Two heads? Will it slobber and make growling noises? He'd seen it all. None of it touched him. He never feared.

So why did his muscles tense? He knew this wasn't real, and yet, an anticipatory calm settled over him. *Because I'm waiting for someone.* And he knew who. He'd had this dream before. Knew who would visit it.

"*Sugar.*" The word, spoken so huskily, whispered all around, and between one blink and the next, Gaston noted Reba in the middle of the dance floor. Looking fetching, he might add, wearing a dress that hugged her top, exposing some cleavage—the kind a man could smother his face against. The skirt belled out loosely, almost touching the tips of her knees. It made him want to inch the fabric upward, tickling those thighs on his way to treasure.

"What are you doing here?" he asked. Knowing it was a dream didn't stop him from playing along with the scene.

"I'm waiting for you."

"Why?" It didn't matter that his subconscious would reply. He wanted an answer.

"You are a puzzle, sugar. Complex and mysterious. Hiding secrets." She tilted her head and smiled. "So many secrets."

"Have you guessed any of my secrets?"

"Maybe if you talked more, I'd know something about you."

"We've barely been in the same room. Makes it hard to communicate."

She whirled away from him, the skirt arcing prettily. "We've seen each other many times, here." She spun and lifted her arms, her face illuminated by a passing blue light. "In my dreams."

"Your dreams? It's you who haunt mine. And I don't think answers I've imagined in this place"—he waved a hand to the empty club around him—"count."

"It's conversations like this that make it so hard to remember why I don't know you when we meet. It feels so real." She took a step and was suddenly right before him, the distance and logistics on the dreamscape following its own kind of science. She placed a hand on his chest. "It doesn't feel like a dream."

No, it didn't. Which was why his obsession worried. The lines of reality blurred, and he liked it too much to care.

He tucked his hand over hers, the skin feeling just as he'd expect—warm, soft, and making even a steady heart like his pitter-patter faster.

What if this was real? What if he'd found a way to talk to her on a mental level? Many cultures claimed they could dream-walk. *Why not me?*

How to test the idea?

"I know how we can figure this out. A code word?"

She understood immediately. "If I say it, then you'll know the dreams are true."

Was it wrong to fear the answer? He leaned close and whispered a word, a word she wouldn't say by accident, a word she would know only if they indeed played together on another plane of existence, one inhabited just by the two of them.

"What an interesting choice," she said, a smile curving her lips. "But I'm not awake yet. Whatever shall we do while we wait?" She rubbed the tip of one foot and dropped her chin, her attempt at innocence so utterly sinful.

And cock hardening. "I know what we can do."

"Always with the dirty ideas." Her head shook. "I like it. But we can't make it too easy." She crooked a finger. "First you have to catch me." Whirling, the fabric of her skirt arcing and flashing her thighs, she took off running, her rich chuckles floating behind, and he couldn't help but give chase. It seemed only right. It was also quite fun.

The blinking lights made it a challenge, as she easily popped in and out of sight. But he'd played this game before—and lost. *This time will be different.* This time, he'd catch her.

A blue light streaked, and there she stood, right in front of him. He lunged, but the light shifted and she was gone. He turned in a slow circle, watching the light bounce. A red spot, and there she stood again, blowing him a kiss.

Turning and turning some more, a green circle of light showed Reba waving. He moved fast, but she blinked out of sight faster.

Why am I playing her game? It hadn't worked thus far. The more he went after her, she more she dodged. She claimed she wanted him to take her, yet she kept herself out of reach.

Time to stand still and let her come to me.

So he did just that, not moving or reacting at all as the light danced and flashed. From the corner of his eye, he caught glimpses of her popping in and out, the frown on her face deepening when he didn't react.

Reba didn't like being ignored.

The light shone right before him, a white beam of light with his lovely lady. He was ready. He reached out to grab her, and this time didn't miss. He drew her close, dragging her on tiptoe that her lips might hover close to his.

"I caught you."

"And what are you going to do about it?" A sultry spoken challenge.

Easy answer. He kissed her. A firm claim of her mouth, her sweet, soft mouth, so pliant against his. The sensual slide of them an electric sensation.

He kissed her and, in so doing, tasted her, felt the warm and wild essence of her spilling over and into him.

And parts of his colder self slipped back. It proved shocking to them both.

She pulled away with a warm gasp. "Surely, you didn't think it would be that easy?" With a laugh and a shove, she pushed away from him, her giggles floating behind as she fled back to the shadows.

As if he'd let her escape. Not now. Not with his blood fired and his body throbbing.

I'm coming for you.

A few steps and the landscape changed. Gone were the club and the lights. He found himself in a forest, the thick-trunked trees casting deep shadows in all directions. At the same time, he could see random rays of moonlight lit some areas, emphasizing the pockets of darkness surrounding them. What surprises lurked? Dangerous ones?

A man could hope.

One of them held his feisty kitten. He caught a flash of movement, the brilliance of her smile as she taunted, "Come and get me." The teasing words came from everywhere at once. He whirled, a full circle while his eyes scanned. The light failed, true darkness fell, and he saw no hint of Reba. Where did she hide? The dark landscape veiled danger. *And I am the most dangerous and dark thing out here.*

The reminder sobered and bolstered a determination to not let that stain on his soul touch Reba. For once, perhaps despite his tarnished aura, he could protect.

I will find you and keep you safe from the perils hiding in my dreams. The fact that he still believed this wasn't real didn't diminish his urgent desire to find her. *I want her. Now.*

He opened up his senses, let the essence of his spirit stretch. *What is out there?* Spectral words whispered on a chill wind.

A rustle of branches to his left. Not her.

A huff of air to his right. Also not her.

His nose twitched at the smell of smoke. Unmistakable and acrid smoke.

There can't be fire. Not here, not with Reba. He'd lost so much already to fire.

This isn't real. I control this. Forget the forest. It didn't exist. He lay in a bed, and Reba wasn't with him. There was no fire, and even if there had been, he had alarms to detect and sprinklers to deploy. He wouldn't lose everything again.

Sleep eluded him, and yet, by his internal watch, it wasn't anywhere close to his usual wakeup time.

Perhaps I heard a noise.

Unlikely. He slumbered safely inside his penthouse condo, the most secure place he could rest in. He should know since he'd set up the security for it. His condo could only be accessed via private elevator, and only he and JF had the key card and code to access. A man could never be too paranoid.

If someone got past his first layer of protection and he did make it to the top floor, they would spill onto a contained vestibule with only a single dead-bolted door into his place. The only other access was the windows, and with no balcony, they didn't seem a likely point of entry.

Then why do I feel heat on my bare skin? Not heat he realized but sunlight, which was odd, as he usually kept the shades drawn tight against the encroaching dawn. Which meant someone had opened them.

Possibly JF since he seemed to have his underwear in a knot as of late.

However, of more concern, was it him, or did he smell the sweet scent of death? He opened his eyes and yelled, "WHATTHEFUCK!"

Chapter Six

"I think you just lost your man card with that girlish shriek," Reba remarked, more than a little insulted. So she was a touch dirty, and smelly, and in his room in the middle of the day because she had a friend who had a friend who loved breaking into places. Really secure places. Was it wrong for a girl to pop in to say hello to a friend?

"You're in my bedroom," he responded, his eyes narrowed in a glare.

"I would have thought you'd be happier to see me." Happier as in flipping her onto her back and taking her lips roughly.

Mmm…yeah…no, that didn't happen.

"Happy? You've got a finger tucked behind your ear like a fucking flower."

"Thanks for noticing." She plucked it out and turned it around. "I kept it as a souvenir from my first graveyard jaunt. Which, I will admit, was less exciting than expected. Not one single walking dead to be seen." Not even a twitch. Such a letdown.

"You're a fucking lunatic," Charlemagne remarked.

"What are you talking about? I am perfectly sane. Three out of five doctors say so."

"What about the other two?"

"They were scared of me." They also moved states. She didn't know why. "And you're one to talk about crazy. Screaming like a little girl, and not so prim and proper anymore." Not with his eyes wild and his hair stuck out all over. The perfectly coiffed gent finally looked rumpled, just the way she liked a man.

My man. Rowr.

"What are you doing here?" he bellowed, probably in a move to reassert some of his manhood—had to do something to counter that shriek. She allowed it, even if she didn't appreciate the tone.

"I am here checking some stuff off my list."

"What list?"

She held up her handheld tablet. "My list of things to learn about you."

"And what does waking me up after breaking and entering have to do with learning about me?"

"First off, I wanted to see if you slept like the undead. Which you don't, by the way. You snore. Not loudly, but, still, loud enough to dispel that theory. And you don't burn in sunlight."

"Why the hell would I burn in sunlight?"

"Isn't that what vampires do? And you don't sparkle either. Pity, I like bedazzled stuff." She wondered if he'd appreciate her vajazzling her girl parts.

"I told you before I wasn't a vampire."

"Yeah, but that didn't mean I believed it." She rolled her eyes. "Like, hello, as if you're going to admit it."

"I am not a vampire or an undead creature."

"And yet your wanker dudes—"

"Whampyr."

"—drink blood." Kind of icky because it was

human blood. Shifters were taught at a young age that humans were not on the menu. And neither were their pets even if they looked tasty.

"As part of their diet, yes, but it's not the only thing they ingest. And they are also not vampires. So don't be thinking of harassing them with sunlight."

It occurred to her that he'd never truly replied to something. "Do you drink blood?"

"Does a rare steak count?"

"Thank God you're not a medium-to-well-done kind of guy. Otherwise, this would never work out." She zigzagged a finger between them, and he looked even more adorably frazzled.

"We are not a we."

"Would you prefer I refer to it as an us?"

He sighed and closed his eyes as he tucked an arm under his head. "It's too early for this kind of logic."

Early? Like, hello, one o'clock in the afternoon. "Is this because I didn't bring coffee?"

"It's because you're wearing clothes. If a woman wakes me, she should be naked."

If I catch another woman waking you or showing any naked bits, she'll die.

But that was getting way off topic. She was here to finish her job. "Since I was in the neighborhood on business…"

"What business?"

"Decoration. There's a horrible condo in the area that is in need of a total remodel. The owner is a single guy, so you can imagine." She rolled her eyes.

"My place does not need help."

"Who said it was for you?" It totally was. Charlemagne's place had far too many yawn-worthy attributes.

"You are not remodeling my place."

"Fine. Live in this boring and dull space, but don't come crying when your creativity shrivels and dies."

"I'll try and contain myself."

"While you're at it, why not also answer some simple questions?"

"Why can't you just leave?"

Leave? But she wasn't done. "I told you, sugar, I have questions. So, stop wasting our time and just answer them. It will be faster that way."

"Or I could kill you?"

She didn't even spare him a glance as she laughed. "No you won't."

"I won't kill you. But I reserve the right to change my mind."

"You're starting to learn." Tick. "And that answers if you're able to learn new tricks."

He indulged in a rather long stare. "I hate to admit this, but I'm curious now as to what else is on your list. Ask your questions."

"Do you bathe in blood like that countess?"

"No."

"Burn at the touch of holy water?"

"I'd demonstrate an ability to gargle it, but who wants to even touch the stuff given people are constantly sticking their dirty hands in it? Speaking of dirty, you smell as if you spent the night with dead people."

"I did. My crew and I visited a funeral home and graveyard. Used coffins aren't a great place to crawl around in for clues. Melly puked. And I got a finger." She waved it.

"Don't tell me more. I don't want to know in case the cops decide to ask me questions."

"If they do come knocking, as far as they are concerned, tell them we spent the night together." Then she hummed a classic '70s porn melody.

The tic woke up in his cheek. "I will not lie to be your alibi."

"You are seriously no fun. And you might want to open your eyes to catch this." She tossed her cross at him, and he snatched it before it hit him in the face. Would you look at that. He didn't start to scream or smoke.

Another check off her list.

"A cross? Really?" He shook his head. "Still not a vampire."

Reba tapped off a few items on the list displayed on her tablet screen. "And you don't sleep in a coffin." Tick. "And you have garlic in your fridge." Tick. "How do you feel about wood?"

At that, he grinned. A wicked grin. A totally evil, evil grin. "I love wood. Why, I'm sporting wood right now. Would you care to see?"

Given he looked rather delicious half sitting in his bed, the covers pooling around his waist revealing a tight musculature that begged for touch... "Yes. I would like to see." Especially since some of the designs tattooed on his body went below the waist. He sported an interesting collection of dark ink art on his body. It made a girl want to trace them—with her tongue.

"If you want a peek, go right ahead." He laced his hands behind his head.

The invitation seemed rude to ignore, but she managed. *No getting involved with him.* She had promised, again, just that same afternoon when Arik commented on her dinner date. *"Don't you dare seduce him."* Or maybe she misunderstood? Maybe Arik employed reverse psychology. Maybe what he really meant to say was jump Charlemagne's bones?

She knew what her biatches would say if she asked them what to do in this situation. She eyed his groin and tilted her head. "How big would you say you are?"

"Is the size of my erection on your list?"

"Nope. That one's just for me." No sharing either. She might not be a dragon with a hoard, but some things a girl wanted for herself.

He uttered a deep sigh. Given she'd been the recipient of many sighs over her lifetime, she ignored it. Not her fault most males couldn't handle the magnificent mind and presence of a lioness.

"Since I'm sure you'll pester until I answer, I am massive."

"Length or width-wise?"

"Both. So now that I've satisfied your curiosity, leave."

"Who says I'm satisfied?" Her girl parts certainly didn't feel satisfied. They throbbed and grumbled for attention. They'd have to suffer; Charlemagne wasn't on the menu. Pity, because she totally craved a bite.

"I'll admit I don't have much experience with shifters. Are all your kind this annoying to speak with?"

"No, I'm just better at it than others. And you're not annoyed. I know when someone is annoyed." It was easy to spot because it usually involved a word that rhymed with punt, and then she did something that got her arrested. Good thing the pride lawyers were good at getting charges dropped.

"If I am not annoyed, then what would you call my mood?" He crossed his arms over his chest.

Hers was aroused, but apparently, he wanted to make this about him. Her sugar was grumpy. But why? A lightbulb lit. "I know what's wrong with you. You're hungry. Let's do breakfast." How did he feel about honey first thing in the morning?

"No eating. I wasn't done sleeping yet."

"Yes you were because you need to come with me."

"Pray tell, why would I do that?"

"Because I need you."

At that statement, his eyes flashed for a moment, a bright red spark igniting in their depths. There one millisecond, gone the next. She might have thought she imagined it, except Reba didn't imagine shit. Her powers of observation were never wrong.

"You do realize, if you need a man, there are services that cater to that."

"But I want you."

Again, he reacted, this time his nostrils flaring as his lips flattened into a straight line. "I am not in the mood to play games."

"A good thing since I always win."

"Is that a challenge?"

"Most definitely."

"And what happens if you lose?"

"Guess you'll have to win to find out." Except, at this point, even she couldn't have definitively said what game they played. But she'd wager it would end with clothes on the floor and one of them on their knees. Probably using his or her mouth and tongue to reward the winner.

"Interesting as your game sounds, I have more important matters to attend to. Please leave." He tried to give it a commanding tone. He forgot one crucial thing.

"I hate to break it to you, sugar, but there is nothing more important than me. And I need you to help me with some business we have in common."

"I already told you no to decorating my place."

"I meant other business."

"I highly doubt that we have any in common."

"So you're not interested in the missing bodies at the morgue then."

"Bodies? What makes you think I'd know anything about missing bodies?"

"Lying?" She clucked her tongue. "Bad sugar." She leaned forward and meant to grab him in a painful hold. A good one when done properly to get some answers. However, he caught her hand.

"What do you think you're doing, *chaton*?" He spoke the words lowly to her.

"I don't like liars. You knew about the bodies. So drop the act. Or I'll forget I'm a lady."

"I should be so lucky." A cocky grin pulled the corner of his lip. "I see there's no point in hiding it. Yes, I know about the bodies. I assume you were checking it out, hence your *eau de mort*?"

"If that means stinky-girl le pew then, yes, that is me and thanks for constantly reminding me." She proffered him a glare. "I didn't have time to shower before coming over."

He offered back a not-bothered-at-all grin. "I didn't say it bothered me, but it is unusual."

"About as unusual as missing bodies from coffins. And we just had a call, the same thing happened at a morgue."

"I still don't see why you feel a need to involve me. This sounds like a human problem." Because everyone knew shifters went for cremation since science had become too strong in the world.

"I don't think this is a thing the humans can handle."

"Why doesn't your king just deal with it himself?"

"He is, which is why I'm here. By commandment of King Arik, ruler of the pride and protector of this city, you are hereby drafted to help with the problem plaguing our citizens."

"He said that?" His skepticism shone through.

"More or less." It had sounded more like, *"Tell him to give us a fucking hand, or else I'll shove his head up his ass."* She might have prettied up the royal edict before delivering.

"Your king doesn't order me."

"But that big council does, and even if they didn't, you'd still help because you know about what's going on."

"I have no idea what you mean." He spread his hands in a false gesture of innocence. "I'm just a simple club owner."

She snorted. "And I'm wearing panties." Look at how his nostrils flared. "I know you're interested in what's happening. You've been keeping an eye on these incidents. Whoever was collecting your information for you was sloppy. Melly followed him back."

"Your hacker out-hacked mine?" He shook his head. "I'll be damned. Very clever."

"You ain't seen nothing yet, sugar. And I will add that you were the one who started this, chasing after my ass."

"It is a sweet ass."

"The sweetest, which is why you're going to follow it and *come* with me." And, yes, she might have winked as she said come.

"I'll admit my curiosity is aroused."

"Is that the only thing?"

He didn't blush, nor look away. He held her gaze. "Why don't you find out?" He leaned right back, stretching his torso. It brought the elaborate tattoos on his body into close relief, their intricate swirls fascinating.

"This isn't me asking you for anything," she noted. "Scientific curiosity only."

"Of course." A faint smile. "By all means, inspect what you'll be begging for."

Naughty man. Always with the outrageous claims. Two could play that game. "With sheet or without?"

"Your choice."

As if there was any choice. She went for skin, of course.

"Did those hurt to get?" She reached out a finger to trace a whorl, but he caught it. "I wouldn't if I were you."

"But you're not me." She reached out again, but he again stopped her hand.

"These marks can be dangerous to those not bound to me. They are meant to protect me from harm."

"So they'll do something if I touch them?"

"Only if they think you're a danger to me."

"And am I dangerous?"

"Most assuredly." He said it with utmost sincerity. A part of him feared her.

Funny thing? She believed him. "Is this your way of chickening out? Are you hiding a teenie weenie under there?"

"I've nothing to hide. And plenty to boast about. Go ahead. Take a look. Touch it, and be sure to mark on your list large, very long, and thick."

"I'll be the judge of that." She'd not truly planned to play with anyone's dick today, especially not Charlemagne's, but if there was one thing a lioness couldn't do it was back down when dared. So her hand went to his lap and groped, with the sheet on. It hid nothing.

Oh my. Oops, she might have said that aloud.

"Yes, oh my, so now that you've satisfied your curiosity, leave that I might dress."

Leave? But the fun had just begun. She grabbed the covers and yanked, revealing him in his naked glory. His hairless naked glory. "You shave your balls?" Perhaps not the most ladylike thing she'd ever said, but she couldn't help it. She was used to the men of the pride. Hairy men who reveled in their fur even when in their human shape. She herself also believed in keeping the curls on her mound intact. But not Gaston. Odd because she'd thought Europeans weren't into shaving.

"I do not shave my pubic region. I am naturally hairless."

"There's nothing natural about that." Just like

the size of him defied explanation. For a rather slim man, he sported a big dick.

The better for spinning on.

As she went to reach for him, he shifted his hips out of the way. "You do realize you still smell like death?"

She wrinkled her nose. "I guess I should shower. Want to come and scrub my back?"

"I am going back to sleep while you make yourself presentable." He actually turned on his side and pulled the covers back over his body.

He ignored her. She almost pounced him, but restrained herself for one simple reason. She was here to do a job. Remember? Arik wanted her to work with Gaston because something wonky was happening in their city, and, for some reason, her boss thought Reba made the perfect liaison. *Take that, Luna. I got my title after all.*

It took but moments to strip and drop her filthy clothes in a pile on his floor. A peek over her shoulder showed Charlemagne not paying attention. He tried so hard to pretend.

"I'm naked," she sang as she pranced into his bathroom. "And wet," she shouted as she turned on the water. She liked to think she could hear him grumble.

She took her time washing, scrubbing all of her parts. Some of them twice. He didn't join her. Didn't even take a peek. Wrapping herself in a towel, she stepped out of the steamy bathroom to see him still in bed, pretending to sleep.

He uttered a grunt when she pounced on him. "Time to get up."

The roll onto her back took her by surprise,

and she stared up at him.

"You should never take me by surprise."

"Why not?" She wiggled under him. "If you ask me, I'm doing okay."

"Only because I didn't truly sleep."

"You wouldn't hurt me." And if he did, it would be the last thing he ever hurt. Some things, like violence to her person, were just never tolerated.

"You should get dressed."

"Says the naked dude on top of me." He might have rolled himself in a sheet when he attacked her, but the fabric begged to be peeled.

"How about we both dress at the same time."

"Why do that? I say we spend the day naked in bed." She pushed her arms out, extending herself starfish style and stretching her nude skin.

He kept his gaze trained on her face. "And what of the morgue business?"

Damn him and his responsible reminder. "Forgot about that. Let's get dressed and get going." At least she'd managed to shower. All day long things had conspired against her having one. First they didn't finish until late with the bodies. Then she might have gotten drunk in the cemetery—which she could now totally cross off her bucket list—and passed out splayed across a fresh mound. Still, though, the shrieking by the old lady was totally uncalled for.

Charlemagne flipped off her onto his back. His sheet cocoon didn't hide the bulge. She sat up, aware she was naked and skin still moist from the shower. "Anyone ever tell you you're too much of a gentleman?"

He'd not tried to grope her once. "I'm a rake

at heart, *chaton*. You just have to ask me for it."

"Let me know when you're man enough to just take." The bold challenge made her movements perhaps a little more sensual than usual when Reba flopped out of bed, tripped, regained her balance without batting an eye, and sashayed over to her giant purse by the chair. She bent over and rummaged—*did he growl? I think he growled.* Me-fucking-awesome. She pulled forth a fresh outfit. Shifters never left home without one—Reba usually went for at least a half dozen. She liked to be prepared.

The red thong went on, flossing between her cheeks without him trying to snap it. A letdown. Did he at least watch? A peek around her body as she bent over to pull her pants over her feet showed that, yes, he did pay attention. Knowing she had an audience added a little more wiggle as she shimmied on her yoga pants. She straightened, chest held proud, only to see he'd averted his head. He wouldn't escape so easily.

Walking backwards, holding her bra over her breasts, she tripped and landed on the bed. Totally what she intended. And why was she suddenly so clumsy around him? "Do up the hooks on my bra, would you?"

She totally expected him to either say no or to grab her and toss her on the bed to have his wicked way. Instead, he deftly fastened her bra and barely touched her. She whirled to tug on her shirt, giving him an ample view of her cleavage in her brassiere before tugging her T-shirt over.

And he didn't touch her once.

He didn't even try.

What a jerk.

"All dressed. Your turn."

As Charlemagne swung his legs over the side of the bed, she didn't move away. It meant she looked up when he stood, way up. For some reason, he seemed taller, so much taller than she recalled. Probably because she was barefoot. She'd left her nasty socks and the mucky running shoes at the door. She'd yet to put on her new shoes. She'd brought some more sedate pumps to change into, the block heel more practical for traipsing around morgues and other places with icky things.

Felines preferred their prey still fresh and alive.

Even better when they run. The chase always left her adrenalized and happy, but her true orgasmic moment came when she pounced.

"Are you going to move?" he asked.

"I'm good."

Gaston stared down at her, a tad disconcerting, so she stared right back.

He blinked first. "You're very bold."

"I am. I'm also bossy and very pride oriented. Mess with my sister biatches, and you mess with me. Piss me off, and after I'm through with you, you'll have to go through them."

"Sounds intriguing."

"If you have a death wish. Messing with any lioness is asking for a shitload of trouble."

"An utter lady until you speak, and even then"—he practically stroked her with his eyes—"you cuss with elegance."

"Thank you." She preened at the compliment. "My mother taught me well."

"I don't suppose she taught you to let a man dress by himself."

"Why would I do that? I've already ogled the goods." She reached around and pinched his ass, a nice firm tweak.

He didn't react. Naughty man. Pretending he didn't notice. A certain part of him that he couldn't control poked her. *Not so calm and cool after all.*

"I am sorely tempted to throttle you so you can't speak."

"I know you're big already. No need to keep implying it." When he looked at her blankly, she might have mimed a big dick blowjob and included choking sounds.

Oooooh. She couldn't contain her glee at the tic that started by the corner of his eye. He was trying so hard to keep it together.

Just a tiny push is all it takes, I'll bet.

He went to move sideways, and she followed and leaned closer. "I've never seen a tattoo like yours before." Shifters had difficulty holding ink. Only certain kinds applied deeper to the skin than the humans ventured ever worked.

"My tattoos are special and not to be trifled with."

"I don't listen well to orders." She tickled her fingers down his arms.

He shivered. No hiding it. "You shouldn't do that."

"Why do you fight it so hard?" she mused aloud. "You want me, I can see that. You flirt, all the time, and make bold claims. Yet, you don't seem to want to take things further than words and teases."

"Sounds like you just described your actions."

"You think I'm flirting with you?" She blinked, attempting her most innocent look. She was pretty sure it fell flat.

"I know you are, and what you don't seem to understand is you're playing with fire. I am not a male to be trifled with, *chaton*."

"What's sha-ton mean?"

"It's French for kitten."

"But I'm not that young."

"Aren't you, because you are a kitten to me, young, immature, and with tiny little claws that might prick and yet do no damage."

The insult actually stung, and she recoiled. How dare he accuse her of immaturity? Sure, Meena and a few others might suffer being childish, but Reba wasn't like them. Not even close. She didn't play games.

At least not often.

Okay, maybe a few.

"You act like you're so much older than me. But you've got to be what, thirty, thirty-five tops." While Reba was hitting the later end of her twenties—where she planned to stay forever and ever.

"I am older than you know." He then gave her the *look,* and in that moment, she believed one thing. She dove for her tablet and tapped at the screen.

"What are you doing?" he asked, leaning closer to look.

"Vampire fact seventeen. Looks forever young. But what about your stamina?"

"Don't start with that again," he growled.

A man of experience. Meow. She wanted to

pounce him more than ever, which was why she, instead, left the room with a parting shot of, "Don't fall over and break a hip getting dressed, grandpa."

Snicker.

Chapter Seven

Old? She left the room because she thought he was an old—decrepit, probably unable to finish—man past the prime of his life. She also seemed to persist in thinking he was a vampire.

Wrong on so many counts. One, he could finish, and more than once a night—and not because he was a vampire. Those creatures were few in the world because they were never as simple to make as people thought.

Gaston also wasn't as old as he implied, but she made him feel old. When he spent time with her, he blossomed. Felt parts of him come alive that he'd not enjoyed in a long time. A real long time. *My existence is boring.*

When had that happened? *I am a world traveler.* A man of experience and means. He owned a club. He made good money. Had a nice place. Could have anything he wanted.

So why do I feel incomplete?

Why am I being such a contemplative sap lately?

With Reba having left his bedroom to wait in the living room, he hurried to dress. Who knew what mischief she'd manage if left alone to her devices too long.

It still shocked him to realize she'd walked right through his defenses. That she could manipulate the elevator? Fine. Electronics had backdoors and could be hacked, just like his front door lock could be picked. Yet, how had she evaded his magic? Why had it not woken and warned him? He'd spent hours crafting those runes and layering those spells.

It wasn't just his household protection spells that hadn't reacted as they should. The tattoos on his body only tingled at her touch. Did that mean he had nothing to fear? Or was the danger she imposed too insidious to register?

Exiting the bedroom, he immediately noted her in the kitchen, hard to miss given her ass pointed straight up as she bent over in his fridge. A pity she chose to wear pants instead of a skirt. The view would have been incredible. He'd gotten only a brief glance in the bedroom. And, yes, he'd looked. He never claimed to be a true gentleman, so he'd watched with much interest as she leaned over to grab her things and then dressed. He would add she flashed him the best sunrise he'd ever seen.

Sounding sappy again.

He gave himself a mental slap and moved into the living room. The kitchen island blocked her from his sight, which meant he could focus on the room itself, a perfectly pristine place. White on white on white. He found the bright purity of it comforting. He allowed black or gray only as an accent. Nothing to jar the serenity.

Apparently, she hated it—which really didn't bother him. Nope. Then again, it didn't surprise him she didn't like the simplicity of his place.

The woman preferred things to scream with vibrancy. Take Reba for instance. She wore bright red. Bright red athletic pants showcasing curved buttocks that rounded the fabric and brought out in bold relief the word, #HOT. She had added a matching athletic sweater over a white T-shirt, emblazoned, *"Too much for you to handle."* Possibly very accurate.

She'd tamed her wild curls into a fluffy tail, which drew attention to her fine features and full lips. Full red lips shiny with gloss.

Damned hot and delicious-looking. He wanted to absorb the bright energy she oozed—while wearing less clothing.

Fight the urge. Fight it because he should be angry at her and, at the very least, suspicious as hell. The last time he'd let his guard down, he got fucked. His sister died, and he lost everything. "How did you get in here?"

"Through the door, of course, silly. Do you have any whipped cream?" She continued to rummage in the fridge.

"Too many calories. And the door was deadbolted."

"You don't really think that stops anyone, do you?" she chided.

True, a real burglar wouldn't be daunted, but what of his other safeguards, his magical runes? They'd never failed him before.

"Did you do anything odd when you got in? Like draw on the walls, sacrifice a chicken, maybe dance naked and call upon a few gods?" He hoped his security camera in the elevator picked it up if she'd done the last.

"And they say lionesses ask the oddest questions. In reply to your questions, none of the above. Although I did bring in a package someone left outside the door."

"What package?" And again, how did it get outside his door? The elevator was keyed to him and JF alone. Either he or his second allowed the team of cleaners in once a week, and they were monitored. Now, it had not only let her in, but some delivery person as well? Time to overhaul the system.

"The package that is on the table in your front hall. It's not all that interesting. I took a peek inside. Just some weird shriveled squirrel thing inside, but huge, like cat-sized."

A desiccated animal? Here? He whirled and headed for the box she mentioned. He flipped open the lid and peeked. Sure enough, what she mistook for a giant squirrel grinned with peeled teeth inside. She'd failed to mention the wings. They fluttered.

Dammit. He slapped the flaps closed, grabbed the box, and took off at a quick trot.

"Where are you running with the dead animal?"

"I'm taking it to my office. And you might want to arm yourself, because it's not dead." As if to punctuate his statement, the box rattled in his arms.

"What do you mean not dead? I saw that thing, and it is most definitely dead. I mean, I've seen fuzzy things in my fridge more alive than this thing."

"Demons aren't like the creatures on our plane." The box thumped again in his grip, the creature inside gaining strength as it siphoned the magic from his wards. That was why he'd never heard them go off. The null demon was feeding on it, and the more it fed, the stronger it got. A full-strength null demon wasn't something he wanted to deal with in his apartment. They tended to leave a mess.

"That's a demon in the box?" Excitement laced her words. "Sugar, you are just all kinds of interesting."

She doesn't know the half of it.

He slapped his hand on the embedded security screen by his office door. He never left it unlocked, and any attempts by someone other than him to open it would result in a nasty surprise. The door clicked and slid open. He immediately entered and dropped the box into the circle drawn on the floor. Something within let out a screech.

Too bad. It was now temporarily contained. Temporarily only because the null creature would be siphoning at the power of the circle, and once it pulled it all in, he'd have to fight it physically. Unless Gaston stopped it now.

Approaching his wall of implements, he eyed the various weapons—swords and daggers, a spiked club and even a crooked wand. Items of magic he'd picked up over the years. Curiosities collected during his travels. Some bought. Some stolen. All powerful in their own way.

He selected a silver-wrought sword, the pommel a beautifully intricate whorl of thick metal that warmed to the grip. The blade shone with blue fire, the Righteous Sword some called it. Perhaps so named because it killed pesky demons.

He crossed to the circle and flipped back the lid on the box.

"What are you doing?" Reba had followed him into the room, and she paced around the outer edge of the circle.

"Getting rid of the pest."

"That seems kind of mean. After all, didn't it just come back to life? Shouldn't we be celebrating a miracle?"

"Celebrate once I've killed it. You don't want it to get loose."

Chirp. The demon gripped the edge of the box and peeked a face over. It blinked large dark orbs right at Reba. Her face softened. "Aah, look at him, Tony, he's just adorable."

He couldn't have said what disturbed him more, the fact that she thought the null demon drawn from the void was cute or the fact she'd nicknamed him Tony. He growled, "I am not a Tony. Tony is an Italian guy who owns a pizzeria. My name is Gaston."

"Yeah, that's not going to work for me because when I think of Gaston, I think of *Beauty and the Beast*, and then I sing that song in my head. You know which one I mean." She hummed a few bars from the tune in question.

He didn't recognize it, but he was sure if he did, he wouldn't like it. Just like he did not enjoy the name Tony. "How would you like it if I called you..." He paused as he tried to think how to shorten Reba rudely. "Ba. As in Baaaa you're a sheep who takes orders from Arik."

She clucked her tongue. "Why would you call me Ba when you're already using *chaton*. We both know *chaton* is the better name for me because I am, after all, such a pussycat."

No, she was a distraction he could ill afford, given the demon had crawled out of the box and now waddled its way toward the edge of the circle in Reba's direction.

"Wook at de wittle baby, taking his first wee steps," she cooed.

"Move back. Don't let it touch you."

"Chill, sugar. You didn't have any pets growing up, did you? I had a guinea pig that was the size of this. Although the zoo people called it a capybara when they took it away. Can you believe they accused my dad of illegally smuggling it into the country?"

She went off on a tangent, and he yanked her back. "You have to listen to me when I tell you this thing is dangerous. And it's going to keep getting stronger if we don't stop it."

"I'm all for hunting deadly things, but I draw the line at wanton killing. Can't we like release it in the wild?"

The null demon reached the edge of the circle and poked it with a finger. The bubble held, but it wouldn't for long. Gaston stepped around the circle, approaching it from the side, his eyes locked on it.

"You better not be about to lop its head off. I just bought this outfit."

"Then step back."

Instead of listening, she peered with entirely too much curiosity at the demon. "Is it growing a tail?"

Probably, given the tails were usually so desiccated once the demons were yanked through the portals that they fell off. They didn't go to waste. A null demon tail was a powerful agent when dried and powdered for use in antidotes.

"You really need to move, *chaton*. We waited too long to act. This is going to get ugly."

Very ugly like its face when the demon

pivoted to grin at him, its teeth pointed black obsidian shards. It hissed, which revealed a second set of teeth, and its tongue lashed out, dripping slobber. The drops sizzled on his smooth concrete, silver-laced floor, leaving corroded pits.

Fuck. He hated when that happened.

Reba finally frowned. "On second thought, I think you should kill it. Probably now. I am not letting him ruin my new Prada Mary Jane pumps. They were a present for not eating that second helping of cheesecake."

"A present from who?" he asked absently as he eased closer.

"Myself. I believe in rewarding me for being a good girl."

He wouldn't mind rewarding her too. Later. Gaston darted forward and swung. The demon moved faster, zipping across the circle then blowing out its tongue, spraying the circle with acid.

More pits in the concrete sizzled, and the circle's aura, the only thing holding the imp, flickered.

He dashed forward again, allowing himself to stand in the center of the esoteric field that he might better pivot and aim. The little bugger ran around the circle, and he could have cursed the size of the restraining ring.

Bigger wasn't always better. Not when a bigger circle meant the demon could remain out of reach.

"Do you need help?" Reba asked, and he could hear the smirk in her tone.

Male pride spoke for him. "I got this."

What he got was annoyed because every

lunge missed, but the little imp didn't, and Gaston cursed as his freshly donned pants smoked. He also didn't have any potions at hand for the critters. Null demons could only be physically beaten. No magic of any kind, not even the most potent of sleeping agents, worked.

"You sure you don't want a hand?" she teased.

"I'm fine," he muttered through gritted teeth.

Something crashed. In another room.

"What was that?" he asked, but he was pretty sure he knew the answer.

"Did I mention there were actually two of those things in the box? I'd wondered where the other one got to."

Crash.

"I guess maybe I should have mentioned it." She shrugged.

"Do you think?"

With an almost audible suction, the last of the circle's magic rolled around the drain and got inhaled into the creature. The demon smiled, two layers of teeth worth. Its wings fluttered.

Fuck. He flung up the sword just in time to deflect the spit. The silver blade flashed blue as it reacted, and Reba gasped. "Oooh. Pretty. Can I have it?"

"I kind of need it for the moment."

He dodged to keep himself between the demon and Reba, a certain odd sense of chivalry making him put himself at risk. No, that couldn't be right. He surely kept himself the imp's target so he could better kill it before it wrecked his condo.

"What's the best way to kill them?" She finally

showed an interest a little too late.

"Decapitation is good."

"Does it have a heart?"

"They have one, but it's down in their pelvis, protected by bone."

"Really? What do they taste like?"

That got him to take his eyes off the demon long enough to cast her a quick glance then do a double-take at her naked body. He'd seen it already. It shouldn't have mattered, and yet it addled him.

"Um…" The distraction cost him. Something bit his leg, and it burned. "Fucking eight-titted hag from hell," he bellowed.

He kicked his leg outward, the momentum not getting the demon to unlatch, but the crack of his pommel on its skull did. The demon unlocked its jaws with a screech of rage and hit the floor. Before Gaston could swing or kick at it again, something with sleek dark fur pounced it.

Reba clamped the creature with her powerful teeth and shook her head. The demon squealed, and acid spit went flying. Gaston leaped out of the way. An answering screech saw Reba lifting her head and turning it toward the door. The imp in her mouth gave a mighty wiggle. She spat it out, and when it hit the floor, she nudged it with a paw. It turned and hissed at her.

She hissed back, her teeth impressive, her snarl vicious, but did he spot amusement in her eyes? The demon scampered off, and he swore. She intentionally waited before padding after it.

Crash. Bang. The sounds of destruction did not make him happy. Exiting his office, he ensured the door closed first before following the noise. He could at least ensure his office remained intact.

The tinkle of broken glass made him sigh, and he sighed again as he entered the living room to see it destroyed. Feathers fluttered around, some still drifting mid-air from throw pillows torn in half. The couch cushions, those remaining on the couch, sported large rips, the foam emerging, the lot of it stained in a brackish-colored blood, blood Reba managed to draw with sharp bats of her paws. It took a minute of him watching before he realized something. "Oh bloody hell, would you stop playing with them already."

With a look that eloquently called him a spoilsport, she pounced on a demon and grabbed it by the head before violently crunching. The other tried to flutter away, the magic in Gaston's place having made it the size of a large dog but no match for a lioness who didn't flinch even when acid sizzled the fur on her legs. One more neck crunch and the second demon was gone. In moments, all that remained was the destruction and the sizzling puddles of goo, emitting the most noxious odor.

Oh and one very naked Reba. "Well, that was fun. And oh dear, would you look at the mess? Everything will have to go. Looks like someone needs an interior decorator to help him fix it."

"You did it on purpose."

An unabashed grin crossed her face. "Yes I did. And you should thank me. Now, care to join me for shower number two?"

He wanted to, which was why, instead, he turned around and stalked off to his bedroom. "I'm going back to bed."

A plan that didn't work out, and thus did he

find himself leaving his place a few hours later for the morgue and not his club. And it took a few hours to get there because that was what happened when you had to deal with a lioness and get out the door. Shiny things distracted, as did puddles of sunshine, food, the thought of food, and basically anything that crossed her path.

Despite being late, he rather enjoyed it all. He'd check himself for a virus later because he was surely sick.

Given the morgue sat on the outskirts of town, he offered to drive. She accepted, but only so she could drive.

Protesting proved futile.

"Give me the keys." She held out her hand, and the other one squeeze him hard, his sac being held hostage. He complied, which was how he ended up as a passenger beside Reba, who drove like a bat out of hell.

A particularly sharp turn, which he was sure saw at least two wheels lift from the ground, had him dryly observing, "We're supposed to be visiting the morgue, not becoming residents for it."

"What are you trying to say? I'm a great driver."

"Ever thought of slowing down?"

"Never!"

"I should have never sent those flowers," he grumbled. Wasn't there a story about a mouse and a cookie? *If you give a lioness a flower, she might think she can break into your place. And when she does, she's going to need...*

Everything he had to offer.

Eep.

Chapter Eight

"So who do you think sent those demons? Think they'd mind sending a few to the condo? I know the girls would love a few to play with."

"You got lucky. Those demons weren't anywhere close to full power."

"And you avoided telling me who sent them."

"Because I don't know. The package didn't have any return address."

No markings at all, just a white label address to Gaston Charlemagne. "Where do the demons come from? And why did they look freeze dried?"

"They come from another dimension. The process to bring them over is what siphons the magic from them. They appear dead. However, if exposed to enough magic, they will revive."

"Like a wilting flower getting some water."

"In a sense. And they are not to be trifled with or dealt with lightly."

"Says the old guy known as Spoilsport."

"You know not what you're dealing with, *chaton*." Tony's arms were crossed, and he purposely stared out the window. Utterly adorable, which was why she kept poking at him to keep the fire of his ire simmering.

"Is the little magician mad because the kitty cat took care of them before he could with his mighty sword?"

"I'll take care of you if you don't behave."

"Anytime, sugar. And bring the sword." A sound rumbled from him, and she bit her lip lest she laugh. "I'm still waiting for a thank you."

"A thank you for what? You brought them into my place."

"And then took care of them."

"Only after they caused a disaster."

"Which I will fix. For a fee." At his glare, she grinned. "I promise to give you the friendly discount."

She slammed on the brakes, given the red light kind of had traffic making it impossible to run.

"I liked my place the way it was." He grumbled, not at all jostled. He'd learned several lights ago to brace himself.

Since she didn't need her hands at the moment, she grabbed his cheeks and pinched them. "Who's being a big baby? Tony is," she sang.

"Your mockery is not appreciated."

"Apparently neither is my ass-saving skills. A thank you would be nice. On the lips." She pouted them in his direction, mostly because she knew he'd recoil. Usually. Not this time.

This time, he grabbed her around the nape and drew her close to him. "You're driving me a little crazy. That shouldn't be possible."

On that she totally agreed. She bit his chin. He shuddered. Shuddered rather violently, which she took as a compliment. He should react when she was near. It was only right.

"Green light." She turned from him and slammed the car forward.

But, apparently, the channel for

communication was open. "What do you want from me, *chaton*?"

"I told you, I want you."

"To help with an investigation in missing bodies. Is that all?"

"Of course not. That's just an excuse. Even if Arik didn't order me, I'd be coming after you. You're interesting, and lucky you, I've decided to stop fighting my attraction." Because, really, if she didn't snare Tony, someone else might, and then things might get bloody. *Better put bleach on the grocery list.*

"Let me clarify. Are you asking me to seduce you?"

Laughter poured out of her. "Oh no. I don't ask. Since you've decided you won't seduce me, I've decided to take you."

"Take me? What is that supposed to mean?"

"In two words? You're screwed two ways. But one of those ways you'll really enjoy." She smiled. It might have held a touch of hungry feline in it.

Meow.

Judging by the line across his forehead, he found himself less than impressed. "I'm not going to be part of your booty call list."

That implied she usually called them back. "It's a short list with one name. Yours."

He stiffened, and she didn't mean just his body. "You're playing with fire, *chaton. Le feu, sa brule.*"

"Burn, baby, burn." She winked. "Admit you're loving this. Us. Look at the fun we're having. Think of the fun we'll have after I make you my boy toy."

He glared.

"Okay, the fun I'll have. Do you know what I'm totally looking forward to? How jealous the girls are going to be when they find out I not only snared the hot weird dude in town but also got to play with demons. Even Luna can't brag she's vanquished two imps from the hell dimension."

"They're not from hell."

"Maybe in your version of events. In mine, they tore a rip through time and space to enter your condo and kidnap you. I, of course, came to your aid and vanquished them." Then came the part where Reba was supposed to claim her prize, but her prize was playing hard to get.

"If you'd not interrupted, I would have taken care of the null demons myself with a lot less damage to my home."

"Are you still whining about the furniture?" She rolled her eyes but still managed to notice the tic jumping high on his cheek. Tick-tock.

"I happened to like that furniture."

"Are you always this uptight on account you're so old?"

"I am not old."

"Says you. But look at the facts, gramps." She fought not to smirk as his tic went into rapid fire. "Antiques and worldly possessions are for those who are stuck in the past and chained to one place. Waste of time when what's important is the here and now." And here was in her car with Tony, wearing her backup outfit since the red tracksuit hadn't survived the demons. The short skirt rode fairly high on her thighs when she sat down. He noticed.

"I'm not wearing any panties," she informed him.

"The demons didn't dirty your thong."

"No, I did. You just make me that excited." She lightly tickled her fingers on his thigh before grabbing the gearshift again.

"Didn't you bring extra pairs like the shoes?"

"What for? I'd rather not be wearing any."

"Well, that must make it easier on laundry day then." He studiously avoided looking her way.

She laughed. "Oh please. I use a service for that. These hands don't do dishes either." She lifted them from the steering wheel—while still going fifty miles per hour—and he didn't even flinch. The balls on him were stupendous.

Totally want to slap them and see them bounce. Off her clit as he took her from behind. Now if only she were the kind of girl who put pleasure before business.

Business. The whole reason she'd gone to his place. She'd gotten distracted for a little bit—pretty, shiny, squeaky toy—but now was back on track. With her head screwed on straight and…yeah. No. She was still just as horny as ever, and he still had yet to do anything about it.

But he would crack. She could tell. "What are you thinking?" she asked.

"More like reading your mind again and the fact you really want to ask me to make you come."

His words startled her enough that the car jumped a lane, but the rapid swerve saved them from crushing the car that didn't move out of her way. "Am not. I'm going to use you and make myself come."

"Why go to the trouble? Just say the words and I'll do all the work. I promise one time with me and you will find me quite unforgettable."

"And yet you're single. Seems like a contradiction."

"Perhaps I've just been waiting for the right woman."

Waiting for fate.

Since when did her feline put trust in fate instead of instinct? And what did her instinct say about him?

Claim him. It was what she should do to make sure no one else tried to lay claim. Her BFFs were all eyeing him except for Luna and Meena. They were too busy ogling their men's asses to notice Tony had them beat.

"I'm not just a woman, I'm a lioness, and we're not afraid to hunt and take what we want," she reminded, dropping one hand off the gearshift to slide up his thigh. Damn it, he tucked his shaft to the right.

"Why take when you can just ask for it? Tell me to make you come. *Tell me and I will make you scream my name in pleasure.*"

The last part of his speech hit her in a soft caress, wrapping around her and dipping inside her, as if he'd spoken to her mind.

"A lady doesn't ask. She waits for a gentleman to seduce." She withdrew her hand and got hit by a wave of disappointment.

"I thought you said you weren't a lady."

"Depends on my mood. But when I'm not, I'm still in charge. I won't beg. And I don't understand your obsession with it."

"Call it a quirk. When we come together, it will be of your volition. I want there to be no mistake after. You will not be able to blame me for what happens."

"And what do you think will happen? Am I going to crave my first cigarette? Am I going to orgasm so hard I die?"

His laughter burst free, loud and genuine. "Your mind truly is unique."

"So is my technique." She gripped the gear knob and stroked it before she hit the clutch and slammed it into place. The car jerked, and it was her turn to laugh. "You are going to love my tongue." She couldn't help the brazen words, never having to try so hard before with a man. Usually a come-hither smile, a wink, that was all it took for guys to put the moves on her—and follow through.

With Tony, he teased her constantly. Made her think he was going to seduce her and have her melt into a puddle of orgasmic goo. It hadn't happened yet. Instead, he'd brought her close to the edge of her own control, and then pulled away.

He teases as well as I do. It meant a constant state of arousal when he was around, and even when he wasn't. Tony had her wrapped around his little finger—and big dick—and they'd yet to even do anything more than kiss and fleetingly grope.

"Just so you know." He leaned over. "I've been told I have a most excellent oral technique."

Growl. Oops. The rumble kind of slipped out, and she might have snapped a, "With who?" Plastic creaked as she gripped the wheel tight.

"Past partners, of course."

Names. Numbers. She'd need them, plus a media manager to notify the ladies Tony was off the market. Until he seduced her at least. "So should I call them for references? I can pull up some numbers for my exes if you want some reviews."

The tic in his cheek almost escaped it jumped so hard, and he turned to look out the window. "I see what you're doing, and I should warn it won't work. I'm not a man prone to jealousy."

"Then it won't bother you to know I dated Pietro, the guy we're meeting at the morgue. It's our past relationship that made him think of calling me about the situation."

"How past is past?"

"Doesn't really matter, now does it, since you just said you're not the jealous type."

His lips flattened, but he didn't concede defeat—he attacked! "Candy, the girl checking in people at the club, has a tattoo on her inner thigh."

"She dies." Oops. Did she say that aloud?

"Possessive much?"

"Yes, and, for some reason, that means you right now." She shot him a glance. "Don't make me pee on you to mark my territory."

"I am more than happy to carry your scent, as it will mean you asked me for pleasure."

"Asking would be wrong, especially since I'm driving and could have an accident." Snort. She'd learned how to drive with Stacey. That biatch knew speed and how to take a corner in her shiny red car.

"Are you telling me you think my touch would make you lose control? How flattering."

He flipped her words around. Point for him. He'd neatly caged her, so she played dirty and spread her thighs.

"Is it me, or is it hot and moist in here?"

"Let me check."

Eve Langlais

He didn't touch her, didn't move a single muscle, and yet, she felt something tickle across her bare nether lips. A ghostly touch. Her legs slammed closed.

A soft chuckle came from him. "You're right. It is hot and wet today."

"What did you just do?"

He wore a smug smile. "I told you I didn't have to touch to make you feel."

So she was beginning to understand. "You have magic, don't you?" Given she changed into a lioness, it wasn't so far-fetched to believe in other powers.

"I have some innate magic, but many of my skills don't need it."

"So you're what? A magician? Do you have a hat with a rabbit inside it?" And because Meena would have asked, she blurted, "And where does it poop? I mean, don't you get worried when you're wearing it that the bunny is getting ready to let some pellets loose?"

"No rabbit and no hat." He shook his head. "Magician isn't quite what I'd call myself, although some of my tricks are about illusion. Others are alchemy based."

"So what do you call yourself?"

He deftly avoided replying by declaring, "We're here."

So they were, the nondescript boxy building not advertising the fact that it served as a city morgue. In broad daylight, standing about three stories and built of brown-hued bricks it didn't look imposing at all, but the lack of parking in the area did pose a daunting task. Reba finally managed to

102

squeeze the SUV in, only needing to give a slight push to the two other cars to give her room.

"Remind me not to loan you the Jag," he muttered as he got out of the large SUV, replete with pushbar in the front and reinforced bumper in the rear.

"I'd prefer to drive your Spider," she remarked, heading to the back of the vehicle and the trunk.

"How did you know I had one?"

"Some of us do our homework." She reached in and rummaged through the bag she'd stashed in the back. A pink hockey bag perfect for carrying her stuff around. She grabbed a baseball bat from inside it.

"What's that for?" He pointed to her gleaming aluminum striker.

"Brain bashing in case we find the bodies and they're not dead anymore." Always best to be prepared.

"I don't know what's scarier, the fact I'm understanding your twisted logic or the fact you think we might run into some dead bodies."

"Don't worry, sugar, I'll protect you." With a wink, she tossed the bat over her shoulder and sauntered into the building, only to get halted by security, who confiscated her baseball bat, despite all her pouting. She might have shown them her less ladylike side, but Tony growled, "Behave," and gave her a ghostly tap on the ass.

It completely freaked her lioness out, enough that she clamped her lips shut. Hard to fight something she couldn't see.

Besides, she wanted to visit the morgue just

so she could say, "I see dead people," except there were no dead people, just a boring guy in a white coat.

"Where's Pietro?" she asked, peeking around for her ex-boyfriend. Because, yes, she totally wanted to see Tony lose it. He would. She'd bet on it.

"Apparently, he's gone on an extended lunch break. I have no idea when to expect him."

"He told us to pop by and take a peek at the missing body situation."

"Are you guys friends with him?"

Reba smiled quite naughtily as she murmured, "Much more than friends not so long ago."

"Gnnggg." Either Tony grunted or they'd just found their first undead body.

Eyes widened behind glasses. "You must be Reba. Shit, you're hotter than he said. Man, is he gonna be pissed he missed you."

"Yes, too bad. But we can't stick around," Tony said, interrupting. "Can you tell us about the missing corpses?"

The guy in the white coat—his nametag said Boring—actually, it was Arnold, which was boring—explained what had happened.

"We had a sudden influx of John Doe bodies, which is people without proper ID, bodies that weren't claimed by family and no next of kin can be found. The funeral home in charge of state burials"—the kind covered by government—"was supposed to come and grab them today. We had five in total."

"Five? That seems like a lot."

"Like I said, it's been a busy week for them. When we shut up for the night, all the fridges but one had bodies." Arnie waved to the wall of metal drawers behind him. "When we came in this morning, they were gone."

"Did you call the police?"

"First thing, of course, and they came by to take statements and dust for prints. But they're saying it's probably just a prank. College boys stealing them for the lab. They're also checking to see if the funeral home came early for them. They seem to think the bodies will turn up on their own."

"Probably moaning and looking for brains."

Arnie shot her a look. "And it's for reasons like that they don't want to make a big deal about it yet. The police are hoping they find them so the public doesn't freak."

Tony frowned. "But shouldn't it be a big deal? We're talking five bodies. Five unidentified bodies that are missing and should have had some kind of image broadcast to try and identify them."

Arnie shrugged. "Usually that's what happens, but not this time for some reason."

In other words, there was something about these corpses the authorities didn't want getting out.

"How were they killed?" she asked. The jumbled voicemail she'd gotten from Pietro early this morning hadn't said much. *"Weird shit over here. You need to check it out. There're bodies missing. PS. I'm missing your body still."* So sweet. Maybe later she'd play the saved message for Tony.

"Initially, they seemed dead by different methods. Strangling, drowning, heart attack, and two unknown causes. Then we opened them up. All of them were missing organs."

"Someone cut them up before they died?"

Arnie shook his head. "That's just it. None of them sported any incisions that could have served as an entry point to remove those organs."

The unspoken question? How did they do it?

"Could their deaths all be related? Perhaps the killer removed them so he could hide his tracks."

"If they were killed, why aren't the police more concerned?"

Reba had a pretty good idea why they were downplaying things. Many a cop wasn't human. Shifters found great stress relief in serving for law enforcement, managing to fulfill that need they had to hunt and chase. Having a lot of shifter-friendly cops on the force meant an ability to fudge over strange incidents. Or ignore them entirely.

"Maybe the bodies have to be missing twenty-four hours before the police can really file a report? I mean, aren't they missing persons?"

The guys both stared at her. What? It seemed logical to her, if you ignored the breathing versus dead body part.

"What's the theory on how the bodies were removed from the premises?" Tony asked.

"There is none. It's technically impossible for the bodies to be gone."

Twitch. Her lioness tail flicked in excitement. Someone had used the word impossible.

I smell a challenge. Ding Ding.

"What did the cameras record?" Tony and his practical questions.

She said kick the human out and she'd put her nose to good use—since someone wouldn't beg for her tongue.

"Nothing was recorded. We checked

surveillance. No one came in or out of this room except for me and Pietro last night, and both of us this morning."

"Which of you was the last person with the bodies?"

"That would be Pietro. He stayed late to work on reports."

"And now Pietro is missing."

Extra-long lunch my ass. The man didn't need more than ten minutes, sometimes even less than that.

As Tony continued to grill Arnie, she paced the room, noting the metal doors. With a yank on the handle, they opened just like on the television shows and held big shelves that could be yanked out. The stainless steel appeared empty, but a sniff brought to mind plastic, antiseptic, and dead things.

Prefer fresh. Juicier that way. Slamming the drawer shut, she checked the others, noting no distinct scent, just a medley that belonged in this place, including Pietro's and Arnie's odors.

But the missing bodies didn't seem to leave much of a smell behind.

She interrupted Tony to ask, "Do the wankers start out in places like this?"

"No. But something else does. I'll tell you later."

Later. Another date. The man was falling for her. He just didn't want to admit it yet.

A crouch down and she peeked at the small grate in the floor, a sniff letting her know it had seen more than its fair share of sluiced icky things. The pipe appeared too small to allow passage of anything bigger than a mouse.

There were windows in the room, the morgue being on the third floor of the building, to her disappointment. Didn't a place that dealt with dead people belong in the basement? It totally messed with the spooky-vibe ambiance.

On the other hand, the place smelled as she recalled the one time Pietro brought her by. Gross with a hint of nasty. The various smells in the room made it hard to concentrate, the storage solutions for the organs and the stringent cleansing fluids permeating the space.

Smells bad. Her kitty lifted its nose in disdain.

Such a snob.

Or... Hold on. Was her pretty kitty giving her a clue?

She looked up and noted several ventilation shafts overhead. "Where do those go?"

"Technically they run all over the building."

"And terminate in the basement?"

"Yes, but you can't mean to tell me you think someone came in through them and stole the bodies back the same way. That's an insane amount of work." Arnie shook his head.

"Is it so crazy? Sugar, you want to give me a boost." When Arnie looked like he might step in first, Tony shot him a glare.

He knelt on one knee and cupped his hands. "He's right. It is unlikely."

"Not really. If they didn't leave by the door, then there aren't many other options to explore." She kicked off her shoe and placed her bare foot in his palms, and as he started to lift, she crooked her other leg behind her. Her arms stretched wide for balance.

The sharp scent of decay became stronger the

closer she got to the ceiling. She braced her hands on either side of the vent, palms flat, and let her nose sniff as she peeked.

"Looks like someone left a hunk of skin behind." The hunk of flesh reeked, making it hard to smell anything else. She shoved at the grate, which moved up into the ceiling space, exposing a large hole. She gripped the edges. "I'm going in."

Tony gripped her foot tight. "No you're not."

"You do realize Arnie is looking up my skirt, don't you?"

The distraction allowed Reba to yank her foot free as she hoisted herself into the ventilation duct. Thank you twenty years of gymnastics. It wasn't just for bone-crushing thighs.

"Get your sweet cheeks back to this room," Tony bellowed. "You don't know what you're dealing with."

"Not yet. But I'll let you know when I find out."

"Come back here. It's dangerous."

"I hope so!" And off she scurried, quite pleased, especially when she found the shaft that went down and she popped in it with a yodeled, "Wheeee!"

The jubilation lasted until she hit the bottom and she finally got to say, "I see dead people." Lots of them.

Eve Langlais

Chapter Nine

The receding scream galvanized Gaston.

"I'll call 9-1-1," Arnold exclaimed, wheezing in excitement.

Cops? Not for this type of situation. "Behind you!" Gaston pointed a finger and, when the morgue attendant turned to look, cold-cocked him, dropping the guy to the floor. Arnold would wake with a headache thinking he got jumped. Meanwhile, Gaston would be long gone from here because he was leaving now. Alone. Apparently, his body didn't get that memo, and it no longer listened since, instead of fleeing out the front door, he went after Reba.

"The things I do for her." And only her. Anyone else he'd say good riddance. Anyone else would have never left his condo alive after the stunt with the demons.

Gaston doubted he'd manage to fit in the ducts as easily as her. Besides, he had a pretty good idea of what they faced, and they didn't like daylight. He took the stairs down, mostly because the lights in the building flickered and he didn't trust the elevator. When he hit the main floor, he ducked behind the stairwell and noted the door marked "Maintenance Only." The lock didn't prove a hindrance. Some tools Gaston never left the house without.

He eased past the door onto a set of metal

stairs, the tread perforated and noisy. Forget a stealthy approach. Usually he would try and hide himself, get a handle on the situation, but given the number of ghouls in this basement utility space, wasting time wasn't an option, especially since the creatures all seemed very interested in Reba. She, on the other hand, appeared to ignore the danger and attempted to speak with one of the ghouls.

"About time you came back from lunch, Pietro. Calling me and then not being here was very naughty of you."

"Gnghgngg."

"Don't you grunt at me. I'm a modern woman. I don't give in to caveman tactics." Slap. She whirled to knock away the hand of a ghoul reaching. "I did not give you permission to touch. Don't make me take a hunk out of you like I did your friend." She took that moment to catch Gaston's gaze, the depths of hers not in the least bit worried, and her smile seemed genuine. "There you are, sugar. I was hoping you'd come find me. I'd like you to meet, Pietro, my ex."

"Grlggng." Pietro squinted one eyed at Gaston and moaned. Actually, all of the ghouls moaned and turned to face him.

"You might want to carefully step around the ghouls and get behind me," he mentioned in the calmest tone he could manage.

"When you say ghoul, do you mean like undead zombie-like creature?"

"I mean like smarter than your average zombie and tougher too." And him without his sword. Good thing he had other tricks—literally—up his sleeves.

"Is the fact Pietro's a ghoul now why you're not more jealous about finding us together?"

"Nothing to be jealous of. You want me. You're just too chicken to admit it."

"Am not too chicken. I already told you I intend to take you. You're the one who lacks the drive to pull a rakish move on me."

"Whatever. Look away from my hand," he ordered. The amulet appeared to fall out of his cuff and dangled on a silver chain. The faceted jewel spun before moving in a pendulum motion.

"Ooh shiny." The ghouls weren't the only ones stopped in their tracks. Reba's lips curved as she watched the swinging amulet.

He needed to remove her. Humans needed only one decent scratch or bite from a ghoul to become the zombies she was so enamored with. He didn't know if the same infection applied to shifters, nor did he care to find out.

The good news was the ghouls were new and not yet too infectious or dangerous, especially since their first instinct was to nest. But as they changed more and more into their creature self, they would crave the flesh of living things.

No one is eating Reba but me.

"Get behind me, *chaton*." The amulet was starting to lose its appeal. Some of the ghouls blinked, their black orbs absorbing the glints of light emitting from the stone.

He thought she would ignore him again, but she skipped behind him, dodging at the last moment the clawing grasp of a hand.

Slender arms slid around him from behind. "Now what, sugar?"

Now for some magic. A finger slid over his ring released a hidden clasp. Powder spilled into his palm. He raised his hand and blew, scattering the dust particles while whispering a word of power, "*Kraahk.*"

The very air ignited, a shimmering curtain of bright white. He grabbed Reba's hand and yanked her in the direction of the stairs. "Climb and don't be slow about it." Because the ghouls were about to get very pissed.

Understatement. Very unhappy, and very inhumane screeches erupted. Reba sprinted for the stairs and climbed them, her bare feet finding purchase. He released her hand instead of following. He whirled and faced the burning creatures limping after him. The flames didn't kill them but rather peeled the human layer from their still forming new frames.

Pale leathery skin emerged, streaked with dark soot. The flames didn't touch them, or burn. He'd have to rely on a different tactic to stop them.

"Pull the fire alarm," he commanded when she reached the top. As the alarm began to clang, he shook something on to his hand. A small sphere, bright yellow and solid. It resembled a gumball.

He tossed it at Pietro, the guy's reflexes too slow to catch it. The orb bounced off the guy's chest. Time to get out of here. Gaston sprinted up the stairs, shouting, "Get outside."

Apparently, she had listening issues. She waited for him at the top, and together they slammed the door against the ghouls, the first of which had reached the steps. Unlike zombies, ghouls knew how to climb. The lock he'd busted meant the door wouldn't remain shut. Nothing he could do for that. Sticking around wasn't an option.

Once again grabbing Reba by the hand, he tugged her out of the stairwell, snaring the guard in the lobby, who yapped in his walkie-talkie. "Move," he shouted, pushing them out the front door of the building to find a small milling crowd of workers, not many given the late hour. "Duck, you morons." The internal counter in his head reached zero, and he yanked Reba down and covered her with his body. For once, she didn't argue.

The ground trembled first, and then came the sound of things cracking and breaking. More rumbling followed as the building they'd just vacated imploded, three stories of brick, metal, and more came tumbling down, crushing anything left inside.

Like ghouls.

Chapter Ten

"We are not buying crossbows for everyone," Arik the spoilsport said.

So unfair. Reba slammed her hands down on the desk, annoyed her king kept shooting down her brilliant suggestions. "Fine, don't order the crossbows and flamethrowers. But don't blame me when you've got nothing to fight the undead with. I've seen them, and they aren't very appetizing." The demon she'd chomped tasted bad enough; the ghoul things she'd encountered the previous day with Tony tasted worse. And, yes, she knew because she bit the first one that tried to grab her when she exited the air vent. All the whiskey in the world couldn't cleanse that taste from her palate.

It didn't help that, once Tony knew, he kept eyeballing her and asking how she felt. She felt fine, until he annoyed her by refusing to give her a goodnight kiss when she brought him back to his condo. He didn't even invite her upstairs.

Probably because I have ghoul breath.

His loss. Just like it was her temper she lost when she tried explaining to Arik, her boss, about the weird undead things that weren't zombies but could make zombies and that shed their skin when ripe. They could be killed, and it didn't always require dropping a building on top.

But that was pretty damned awesome. Tony had

some pretty cool secrets hidden up his sleeves. A better one hidden in his pants. Tony was a hell of a lot more interesting than listening to Arik who lectured. "Blah blah blah, stay low key"—ha, as if—"don't destroy city property." Talk about ruining a girl's fun. "Don't get involved with Charlemagne." Too late, Reba had him in her sights.

Arik really should spare his breath. All he did was spout boring warnings she had no intention of paying any attention to. Then Arik compounded his gaffe by refusing to entertain the list of weapons she recommended—a list garnered from religious watching of *The Walking Dead*. Although, she had to admit, the spiked mace suggestion was all hers.

Snap. Arik's fingers clicked in front of her. "Pay attention."

"I was. You want to take away all my fun time." She pouted, but it didn't work on her boss.

"I want you to be careful. It sounds like there is some weird shit happening in our city, and I don't want us to get caught in it more than necessary."

"We are caught because it's happening on our turf."

"Which is why we're going to keep monitoring the situation. You said something about Charlemagne recognizing these creatures."

"Like I was saying, they're called ghouls. They're made from some like magic ritual and a bite or scratch from a mature one is what makes zombies."

"And before those ghouls, we had those bat dudes eating up some folk."

"Don't forget the demons I pulverized."

"I'm seeing a pattern emerging, and it all

seems to center around Charlemagne."

"I know. He's like the coolest boyfriend ever." Too late she realized what she'd said, out loud. Maybe she did need a filter, but then she wouldn't inspire such consternation on her boss's face.

"Boyfriend?" Arik's brows pulled together. "What did I say about not getting involved?"

"Don't get caught?" Actually, that might have been his instructions to Luna.

The king of the pride sighed and leaned back in his chair. "I don't suppose there is any point in telling you to stay away from Charlemagne."

"He's interesting."

"I should have had the man killed when he first showed up," the lion pride king muttered.

Except Arik wasn't a killer. At least not a wanton one. He knew, in order to keep the pride out of trouble, they had to not cause trouble. Or at least not cause trouble out of the ordinary. Bar fights totally didn't count.

"I don't think Tony is the one we need to worry about." But she worried about him. Someone had, after all, sent those demons to his house. She would have to keep a closer eye on him, which was why less than three hours later—a record given how long it usually took her to choose and pack clothes— she was on her way through the lobby of the condo the pride owned, a train of suitcases in tow—only three since it was just for the weekend. She didn't pass unnoticed.

The main area was occupied by couches and, on those divans, lounged a group of lionesses—in human shape. They were told by their alpha no pussy in public after the third time wildlife animal control showed up looking for lions and tigers.

"Where are you going?" Melly asked, popping up and leaning her chin on the back of the couch to watch.

"Spending the weekend at my boyfriend's."

That got a chorus of "ooohs." And someone fell off the couch.

"Some of you might have heard of him. Gaston Charlemagne." And yes, she loved how his named rolled off her tongue. Once he stopped being so stubborn, he'd feel her tongue. But despite her taunts to him, she wouldn't give in first. A man should seduce a woman. She just wished he'd hurry up before her girl parts shriveled up and died.

"Since when are you hooked up with the vampire dude?"

"He's not a vampire—" she began to say.

"Bummer for you."

"—but a sorcerer."

"He doesn't look like Gandalf," someone observed.

"Must be some kind of magical wand," snickered another.

Reba smirked. "Oh baby, you should see the size of his wand. And it's magically delicious." With blown kisses, she left her crew. They knew to follow the action on Twitter.

Since she didn't have wheels—on account they got impounded as part of some investigation into the stealing of a dried sample of ancient catnip at the botany museum—she hailed a taxi. The cab driver dropped her outside Tony's building. Tony wasn't waiting for her. Perhaps he didn't read minds after all.

Slapping her card against the reader—the price she'd paid the hacker to get the keycard plus the code totally worth the trade of her Louis Vuitton bag. Melly's services didn't come cheap—she managed to heave and ho her luggage into the body of the elevator. Then she manhandled them past the door of his condo. At least Tony had not bothered changing the locks, but she noticed he'd decorated the walls flanking the entrance into his place with swirls of red paint, violent slashes, and strange letters, the markings still dripping wet.

So much for not liking color. She wondered when he'd done that. Given it was early evening and the lights were on inside the door, she yodeled, "Sugar, I'm here." Let the game of flirtation begin.

She entered his condo, only to stop dead. It had nothing to do with the fact that the place looked as pristine as the first time she'd seen it. What perturbed her was the woman standing by the window, a stunning woman who turned when she saw Reba and smiled. A very sweet smile, for a petite and ethereal-looking girl who, when asked, "Who the fuck are you?" announced, "I'm Vivienne, Gaston's fiancée."

Chapter Eleven

"You're watching for her again."

"No, I'm not." Lie. Gaston totally watched for Reba and expected her to appear. A part of him really wanted her to come find him. They'd parted so abruptly the night before, mostly because he needed to gather some things from his office that he might deal with any ghoulish surprises that might have survived the building collapse. He spent a long night, out of sight of first responders, scanning the ruins of the morgue and ensuring nothing crawled from the debris.

A part of him went home expecting to find her in his bed.

It proved empty. So he slept slightly, expecting at any moment she'd wake him. He spent a fitful night and morning dozing in and out of sleep. She didn't appear.

Didn't even call.

By the time he went to the club, he was checking over his shoulder, certain he'd spot her shadowing him. Lionesses were known for their stalking skills. Alas, no one pounced him. No one even hunted him. *Surely she didn't give up so quickly?* It seemed suspicious, and he almost managed to justify going after her himself as the hours passed and he didn't catch a glimpse of her.

Don't tell me she's done with me. He wouldn't

allow it. Couldn't. Between his dreams and real life, he'd become very invested in Reba. He couldn't live without her, and that very simple truth, a truth he couldn't ignore, brought something into glaring view. She'd bewitched him. Obviously, or he'd inhaled something he shouldn't have, which was why he found himself obsessed with the woman.

Gaston Charlemagne did not chase after women. Not even this woman. No matter how much she attracted. No matter how many times he chased and caught her in dreams.

How to fight her allure? When she was around him, she shone too brightly for him to ignore. So he tried to concentrate on the things he didn't like.

She was a feline. Bloody arrogant creatures, always shedding and doing their claws on the wooden furniture. A cat who would probably purr at the right stroke.

What about the fact that she had no common sense? Facing down ghouls as if they were simply regular pests, even taking a bite out of one. Her fearless nature made her only more desirable.

Just like her absence made him only more anxious the longer it went. Over twenty-four hours now at this point—not that he'd counted. He wouldn't break and find her first. He truly believed she would come to him, which was why he'd sent a memo out to his staff that she was to be allowed access to the club with no wait. No point in getting in her way. What Reba wanted, Reba got.

Now if only she wanted him as much as he wanted her.

His lust for her grew the more time they spent

together, but in equal measure grew his consternation. He didn't have time for this kind of complication. The signs of his enemy's presence sprang up all around him. Things would only get more violent.

As if the threat of violence would deter Reba.

Bang. The door to the office swung open and hit the wall. A very feisty-appearing Reba stood framed in the opening, her short yellow summer frock clinging to her cleavage before falling in a loose bell around her. She wore Roman sandals on her feet, the laces crisscrossing over her calves. Could he declare himself a loser right now and throw himself at her feet for worship?

Reba wagged a finger in his direction. "Don't you try and caress me with your eyes, sugar. I am very cross with you. I thought you and I had something going on."

"We do." Even if they shouldn't—make that couldn't—quite yet.

"Don't you deny—hold on. Did you just agree?"

"There is something between us, *chaton.* Lying isn't going to make it disappear."

"Funny you should mention lying because that reminds me why I'm so cross with you. I told my crew I was staying with you this weekend, but—"

"Hold on a second, you're staying with me? When was that decided?"

"After my meeting with Arik, it was determined—"

"By your lion king?"

"No, sugar, by me, that I need to keep you in my sights because you have interesting things happening around you. And you also have secrets that I intend to discover."

"A man never divulges everything." Secrets were power.

"Yeah, well, you should have divulged the fact you weren't available." Her lips pursed, and her eyes flashed.

"What are you talking about?"

"Don't play innocent. Care to explain who the hell Vivienne is?"

The name snapped him with the impact of a slap. "Where did you hear that name?"

"From the hussy's mouth."

All of the blood drained from his face. "You met her?"

"Yes I met her. Tiny little blonde thing. Rather puny-looking if you ask me. I would have expected you to enjoy a more robust paramour."

"Where did you see her?"

"Getting pretty cozy in your place. You never mentioned a fiancée."

"Because I severed the relationship a long time ago." And then spent the next several decades of his life hunting down her hidey-holes and burning them to the ground. Tit for tat. Only she seemed to escape each and every time. So he found her, again and again. Or she found him and pretended as if he was still young, stupid, and in love.

"Are you telling me the cow is stalking you?" Reba's expression brightened. "Well, that puts a different spin on things. Don't you worry. I'll fix that for you, sugar." Reba whirled, her bright skirt flaring, showing a peek of curved mocha buttock.

He blinked as he realized what she'd

proposed. "No!" He shot out a hand, and though he stood across the room, the door slammed shut and stayed shut, despite Reba's determined tugs.

Amber fire sparked in her eyes as she whirled to growl, "Let me out. I have a blonde mousie to catch and warn away."

"Leave Vivienne to me."

"Remember when I said I was the jealous type?" Reba took a step toward him. "I wasn't exaggerating. I am super possessive. Especially where you are concerned. So I feel it only fair to warn you that I'm going to probably shave your ex's head, and eyebrows. Then I'm going to explain, probably with my fists, how you're not available. I don't share my boyfriends."

"Since when am I your boyfriend?" He took a step toward her. "Are you finally about to beg me to pleasure you?"

"I was thinking about it, but I figure you're not far off from seducing me." The coy wink almost made his capitulation a certainty.

"You don't control me, *chaton*."

"Are you sure about that?" She strolled into the room, only to lean against the glass, the strobe lights outside illuminating and shadowing her frame at the same time.

Reba certainly had him mesmerized. His gaze tracked her every movement. A hard part of him throbbed, the need strong to bury himself inside her.

At this point, he wanted to be the rake she wanted. To ply her with kisses until she melted then tease her soft flesh until she came apart in his arms. He'd finally reached his breaking point. And yet...

Seduction would have to wait. The game he

played with Vivienne had entered the next level. Things would get dangerous from here on out. What surprised him was Reba escaping Vivienne's clutches.

"If you saw Vivienne at my place, then how come you're here? She wouldn't have just let you leave." Vivienne wasn't one to waste an opportunity to strike at him.

"She actually encouraged me to go. Said to give you her love and tell you she looked forward to your reunion." Reba's lips twisted. "For that alone I almost brought you her heart, but the authorities frown on the carrying of organs in the city, especially if they're not in a special cooler meant for transplant. And, no, I'm not explaining how I know that," she said with an ominous undertone.

So Vivienne let her leave. What devious plot did she weave? Because his former paramour wasn't usually known for being nice. Especially to Gaston's lady friends. "What were you doing at my place?" No point in asking how she got in. Apparently, locks didn't prove a hindrance.

"I told you. Bringing over my stuff for the weekend."

"Without asking first?"

She rolled her eyes. "That would have ruined the surprise. Given all the fun stuff happening lately, and I don't just mean ghouls and demons, I thought I should stick close."

"How close?" he asked, stepping toward her, knowing she probably didn't wear panties under that skirt but still feeling a burning desire to check for himself.

"As close as I can get. Think skin to skin. I forgot my body pillow, so I was planning to use you to sleep."

"Sleep? Do you really think we'll get much sleep together in my bed?" He stopped in front of her, a man entranced. The scent of her, vanilla cinnamon, tickled his senses, and the hands he placed on her hips filled with her curves.

"What are you doing?" she asked in a husky murmur.

Seducing, which he'd sworn not to do. He couldn't stop, though. He drew her to him and began to sway. "I'm dancing with you."

"We can barely hear the music."

Indeed, the soundproofing allowed only the barest pulsing thump of bass to penetrate. He didn't care. The song he wanted to dance with Reba sang in his blood.

"Close your eyes and imagine it." His hand spanned her lower back while his other cupped her nape, drawing her near. "Feel it pulsing in you. A steady beat." He rocked her body with his. "Can't you feel it?"

Her hands curled around his waist, and her thumbs tucked into his waistband, her lower half pressed against him undulating so deliciously. "Yeah, I feel it."

How could she miss it? His erection pulsed, following its own rhythmic chant. Swaying in time to a song only their bodies could hear, they slow danced, bodies pressed, swaying and moving, the heat between them rising. Her face lifted, her shuttered gaze meeting his, her lips moist with invitation.

Surely it wasn't seduction to kiss that offering? He let himself lightly brush her mouth, only the lightest of touches. Her staggered warm breath fluttered in reply, and her fingers dug into his hips.

They both fought so hard to remain in control, and for what? So he could spend one more night with blue balls and an empty bed?

"Fuck it." The expletive left his lips and he whirled her until he could press her back against the glass. With her firmly braced, he stopped playing games and truly kissed her. Kissed her hungrily. Passionately. Their teeth and lips clashed in a hot duel of breaths.

With a growl rolling from Reba's lips, the room spun, and he was the one pressed against the glass, her greedy mouth sucking at his lower lip.

"What are you doing?" he asked.

"Taking you."

"Too late. I'm going to have you first."

He grabbed a handful of her wild and awesome hair, the crinkly waves of it crushed in his fist as he bent her back that he might nibble the column of her throat.

She uttered a husky moan of pleasure then murmured, "Fire."

Yes, fire. He burned with need for her. His desire danced hot as a flame.

And yet, she cooled, her body losing its relaxed sensuality, and her next words killed what remained of his ardor.

"Sugar, your club is on fire."

What? He broke her embrace to stare out the viewing window and spotted the orange glow of flames, contained for the moment in the garbage cans he kept scattered around the place. No big deal. His staff would extinguish them.

One of the burning bins was tipped over, and liquid fire, born of alcohol, ignited as it spread across the floor. He couldn't hear the crackle or smell the burn, but he could see the effect by the open mouths, the silent screams as people noticed the peril then the panic in their faces, especially once the flames found fuel. Spilled drinks, dropped napkins, it didn't take much to feed the hunger of one of the deadliest elements.

Alarms went off, screaming a warning to patrons and staff to get out. Sprinklers activated, soaking everything in one half of the club. The other half, the half he was in with Reba, still burned.

Always with the fire. The work of his enemy.

"I'm going to take one guess and say this is the work of your ex-girlfriend," Reba snapped. "I see she's just as bad as my cock-blocking crew. The nerve, interrupting a girl before she's done."

"We perhaps have more problems than our pleasure." The smoke curled outside the window of the office, and while it didn't yet creep in, they would have to exit shortly or perhaps find themselves extra crispy.

"Don't worry, sugar. I'll save you."

She went to open the door, only to yelp as she pulled her hand away from the knob. "Ouch! That's hot."

Probably because the flames already licked at the steps, the wood and metal no match for a determined fire. The smoke billowed in, choking and thick. His eyes watered, and even his tough *chaton* coughed.

He wasn't about to die today, and neither was Reba.

Going down the stairs wasn't an option. Even if they made it past the flickering flames to the bottom, he doubted they'd make it outside before the building succumbed. Already metal creaked and groaned. Glass smashed next. He peered upward at the skylight, blacked out with paint, except for the section smashed wide open. Jean Francois peeked his head through and spotted Gaston through the thick swirling smoke that sought escape.

"Catch."

A single strand of rope was tossed, and Gaston snared it one-handed. Chivalry said, ladies first. Self-preservation said, save himself.

"Hold on to me," he told her, wrapping the rope around his forearm. She didn't have to be told twice. Reba wound herself around him, arms around his neck, legs around his waist—she definitely wore no panties. The stairs creaked, the landing he stood on swaying under his feet.

He leaped, and for a moment, they hung suspended in mid-air, and then gravity tried to suck them down.

The jolt to his arm caused him to grit his teeth. The pain proved intense. But he'd lived through pain before.

He breathed a word of power. *"Luuxkaeli."* Immediately, the pressure on his arm eased, and they quickly ascended, JF yanking them up and through the skylight. "Nice timing," he acknowledged as his feet found purpose.

"Buy me a drink later. We need to move."

It was a dash across the rooftop, and all the while the building trembled, especially once the fire reached the alcohol behind the bar and things started to explode.

Jean Francois leaped across first to the next rooftop, his wings fluttering and giving him an extra-long glide. He turned and was ready to catch Reba when she soared, legs peddling madly. Then it was Gaston's turn to jump, still light as a feather, which meant, when Reba tackled him and said, "That was fun," he hit the roof hard.

"Oomph."

"That was epic. Totally Indiana Jones cool. Better. Never a dull moment with you, sugar." And then she kissed him. With tongue.

JF almost died when he interrupted. Then again, he did have a point, "Now is not the time to have your white ass being video taped humping when the media copters arrive."

True. And Gaston soon had more to worry about than his club being burned to the ground. It seemed his condo had suffered a fiery fate too.

Homeless and blue-balled. Could his evening get any worse?

Chapter Twelve

This evening sucks! She blamed it on cock-blockers. Everywhere Reba turned people were trying to keep her from doing the horizontal tango with Tony. From the club catching fire to the bat dude, who observed that perhaps they shouldn't be making out on the rooftop, then grumbled when she tried to start things up again with Tony when they got to the ground.

The prude mumbled something about obscene acts. *I wish we'd gotten to the obscene part.* Then maybe she wouldn't be so horny all the time. She seemed to suffer from tingling girly parts since she'd met Tony. There was only one cure for that.

So when Jean Francois—with a gruff voice and surly attitude—told Tony he could stay at his place, she dove in and said, "He's staying with me."

"That's probably not a good idea," Tony observed. "Being with me will attract danger."

"You're right." She tapped her lip with a finger. "I should go home alone. Vivienne is more likely to follow me that way."

At that remark, his lips flattened. "She's after me. Not you."

Reba sidled close to Tony and grabbed his ass as she nipped his earlobe. "She's a jilted ex-girlfriend. I guarantee she wants a piece of me. Which is cool, I wouldn't mind bitch slapping her a bit. Someone needs to teach her how to let go." Because Tony belonged to Reba now. She just needed to place her mark on him to make it clear. To do that, she needed alone time with him.

"The woman will be safe at her condo. They have adequate security in place," Jean Francois—a name she couldn't help but repeat with a snooty air in her mind—remarked.

"Adequate for shifters and humans, but not for someone like Vivienne." Tony scrubbed a hand through his hair. "I should go with her."

"What of the police?" asked Tony's second-in-command.

"I've already given them depositions. They are treating both incidences"—because the club wasn't the only victim of fire—"as arson and are investigating. If they require me further, then they can wait until the afternoon. I am not going to lose sleep over this. No one died."

This time. But that was only pure luck. If Vivienne kept attacking, someone would get hurt, or die. Most people might have been scared by this knowledge.

Reba got adrenalized, which was why she dragged Tony back to his car—a sleek gray Mercedes today—and gave him directions on the fastest route to her place—which involved a few turns into alleys that had him growling, "Can't we stick to roads?"

"But this is quicker," she replied. And speed was of the essence. Her lady parts were in danger of dying!

Parking in the garage below the condo complex meant missing the folks surely still lounging in the lobby, even at this hour. They made it to her condo without issue or interruption.

Everything was going well until she shoved him in the direction of her bedroom. He stopped in the doorway, tight-lipped and silent. Probably overwhelmed at the fact that he'd lost the game they played and would now seduce her.

Or it could be he was angry that not only had his club suffered thousands of dollars in damage from the fire someone intentionally set, but his apartment, his lovely apartment that played host to her designer shoes and irreplaceable Louis Vuitton bag, had also suffered a pyro fate. *Sob*. He was right to be somber. She could never replace those items, and one person was to blame for their loss.

A psycho ex-girlfriend who thought she could get in Reba's way. Hell no. Vivienne might have been busy, but she'd never messed with a lioness before. Bad move. Bye-bye, Vivienne. Once Reba got her claws in the woman, there wouldn't be anything left for the cops to find.

I'll make her into a julienne meat fry. Time for Vivienne to disappear. Permanently.

Amidst all the destruction, there was a silver lining. Look who was only feet away from her bed. Now if only he'd start stripping and get to work. Instead, he decided to talk.

"Your bed is tiny." He glared down at it.

He should treat it nicer. We're going to spend a lot of time in it. Because he would seduce Reba tonight. She had a feeling...it started below her waist.

She ran her fingers over the bedspread and tugged the chenille comforter. She liked cuddly things and hard things that needed cuddling like Gaston. "My bed is a double, on account I needed room for my wardrobe." The walk-in closet and second bedroom had run out of room. Some people said Reba had a shopping problem. Some people should mind their own business before she punched them in the face. "But don't worry, we'll both fit. I'll sleep on top."

"And where does that put me? With the dust bunnies under it?" A rather pointed arch of his brow gave him such a rakish air.

"Silly sugar, I keep my winter coats stored under there. I meant you get the bed and I get on top of you. You'll be my mattress." Was it too soon to ask him if he slept in the nude? She hoped so because she really liked skin-to-skin contact.

His jaw tightened. Actually, all of him tensed, and she realized something. *Oops, I spoke out loud again.*

A shake of his head as he said, "I don't think this will work."

"Are you accusing me of being too heavy?" She planted her hands on her hips. "Is this your way of saying you think I'd squash you?"

"You know you're fucking perfect."

She might have thrust her chest out a little at the tersely given compliment. "Would you rather we spoon?"

"Very much, but we won't. Not yet. This was a bad idea. I can't get involved with you, not until I deal with Vivienne."

"Don't you worry about that blonde psycho. I'll take care of her."

He spun on her and gripped her arms, his expression intent. "Don't go near her. You have no idea what she is capable of."

"Lighting a match apparently. How about we

see how she does when she has to deal with my fist?"

"You will stay away from Vivienne. Far away. She is far more dangerous than she appears. Her influence with my whampyr staff and her direct attacks are only the beginning. It will get worse, much worse. This isn't the first time we've fought."

"If she's so nuts, how come you haven't wiped the floor with her yet?"

"A few times I thought I had. There should have been no way to escape the last trap I set for her, yet here she is. Again."

"Sugar, I think you just spouted the plot for a few horror movies I've seen. Is she going to turn into a giant-ass demon bitch lobbing balls of fire at some point?"

He blinked at her.

"I'm going to take that as no then. And I assume she's mortal?"

"What else would she be?"

"How the hell would I know? Since meeting you, I've encountered bat dudes and ghouls. And you're a magician."

"And you've only scratched the surface. You have no idea what creatures she can command."

Reba shrugged. "So she's got some pets. We took care of the ghouls, and you took care of the wankers she converted. She set fire to a few things. Insurance will cover it, and hey, no one died."

"Except for my fish."

Her turn to bat lashes. "I'm sorry for your loss."

For a moment, they both stared at each other. The laughter emerged at the same time and with lusty insistence. "You are completely ignoring what I'm saying."

"No, I hear you. Your ex-girlfriend is going to make my life hell. Sounds like an episode for Jerry Springer. However, in case you hadn't noticed, I'm not easy to scare. You have met my biatches, right? This kind of shit might be a little more heebie-jeebie than usual, but I'm not going to walk away."

"This isn't a game." The words snapped as his face darkened. "The stakes are real. People will get hurt. People always get hurt. And sometimes it's my fault."

"Sometimes good guys have to do bad things."

"Are you calling me a good guy?" He sounded quite incredulous.

With good reason. "Oh no, sugar, you're a bad boy, through and through. It's one of the hottest things about you."

"Everything that comes out of your mouth is hot."

She couldn't help but utter a husky laugh as she purred, "Things get hotter if you put them in."

Flames born of erotic tension practically snapped between them. The temperature definitely rose.

"You are a temptation I should ignore."

"Fuck ignore. Let's be the evil power couple who takes the fight to the enemy and doesn't take any names."

"How did I ever think you were a lady?" His fingers brushed her cheek. "You're a fucking queen."

"And who will serve me?"

His fingers curved around to the back of her neck, splaying and holding her. "The right answer is you will service me. But…" He brought his mouth close and whispered the next words against her mouth. "What I really want is to feel you come on my tongue."

As if she'd argue with that.

"I would like that very much. But shouldn't we shower first?" A patina of smoke covered them, but he shook his head.

"No more waiting." He flipped her onto the bed and pushed her knees apart that he might stand between them. "You wanted seduction." He dropped to his knees and slid his hands up her thighs. "You win."

"That seems too easy."

"Too easy?" His eyes smoldered as he caught her gaze. "You've haunted my every waking and sleeping thought since we met. Tortured me without even trying. This is long overdue."

"You dream of me?"

"Every." His hand slipped higher. "Single." And higher. "Fucking night." He leaned forward, and his mouth pressed against the inside of her knee, such an innocuous spot, and yet, as he slid his lips past her knee to her thigh and further, pushing the fabric of her skirt as he moved, she found herself holding her breath. Every part of her tingled. Shivered. Tensed in anticipation as her skirt rose past her mound, baring her to his view.

"This lack of panties is most distracting, you know." He blew on her.

Her intelligent reply? "Ungg." Yeah, he blew hot air on her moist lips, and she could barely remember her name. She knew his, though. "Tony."

"What is it, *chaton*?"

"I want it."

Warm air swirled on her nether lips, and he rubbed his mouth against her, teasing the flesh. "You don't have to beg."

"I'm not." Before he could realize her intentions, she'd flung herself at him and pushed him to the floor, straddling his waist. "I'm just being proactive about what I want."

She wiggled down his body, her hands tugging at his clothes, baring his shaft. It sprang free, fierce and proud and delicious. She grabbed it and popped it into her mouth for a lick. Mmm. She did so love to lap at things, and she would have happily licked until she got to the creamy center, but she found herself rolled onto her back.

"I am the one seducing here," he growled. He crouched between her legs and found her heated core, plying his tongue to her swollen flesh and making her pant. He touched her just right, his tongue flicking one moment against her clit, the next pushing into her, teasing her channel.

Her need to have him inside her had her rolling them again, her mouth latching onto him to ensure he was just as wet and wild as she was. He was wilder. She was on her back again, and this time, his mouth clung to hers hungrily, and fingers parted her lips below. He thrust them into her, and she arched, letting loose a cry into his mouth. He lay on his side, and she turned, managing to grab hold of him and tug at his turgid length. For every stroke she gave him, he gave back, his fingers slippery with her cream, their hips undulating in unison. The breaths ragged between kisses. She'd waited so long she didn't care if he just fingered her. It felt good, felt great, and she couldn't hold back. Her flesh quivered, her channel clung, and she came. And came, waves of pleasure rocking her body, making her hum, but her body didn't feel fulfilled.

She needed something more.

"I want to claim you," she whispered against his lips.

"And I will allow it," was his murmured reply. "But only once I get rid of the danger to you."

"Allow? Oh, sugar. That's not up to you."

"See you when you wake."

"What?"

A fine dust filtered down, and she couldn't avoid sucking it in or hearing his whispered, "*Noctis.*"

Chapter Thirteen

As Reba's eyes closed, succumbing to the sleeping agent, Gaston groaned, mostly in frustration. Not only did she still pulse against his fingers, her climax still riding her flesh, he throbbed too. He'd not achieved the same kind of release. He wouldn't allow himself that, not while he had unresolved business.

It seemed too selfish, even for him, to allow himself a moment of pure bliss when evil courted the city. So many could die, even more might resurrect as something else, and he had to stop it.

The nobleness of it made him want to gag. *I'm not a hero.* So why did he persist in acting like one?

He stroked her soft cheek, noted her soft and even breath. The living color of her skin. The even more vibrant hue of her aura.

She is why I must leave. It proved harder than he expected. He allowed himself a quick wash, a rapid sluice to remove the grime and the scent of her on his fingers. That was truly sad.

He'd brought up a bag of clothes that he kept in his trunk. It wasn't just shifters who traveled around with spare sets. Clean and attired in under seven minutes, he allowed himself one more gaze upon Reba, and a soft kiss, not of goodbye. *I will be back.*

But first he had to kill something. And that

something couldn't be anyone in her pride. He'd no sooner left the condo and waited for the elevator when a pair of doors opened and bodies slunk out. In mere moments, he found himself surrounded and watched. Ever wonder what it would be like to have a half-dozen wild eyes regard you and assess you? Ball shriveling, but he didn't let their excellent intimidation show. These types of personalities respected only one thing—insouciant brashness. "Can I help you, ladies?"

"Ladies?" Snicker. Stacey eyed him. "You're looking a lot better than you did when you arrived."

The athletic Joan leaned close. "Freshly showered."

"But only after being naughty," added Melly.

"That was fast." Joan's nose wrinkled. "Poor Reba."

The tic started, and despite knowing it was a rabbit hole, he still felt a need to reply. "Reba is perfectly fine."

"Fine? Like I said, poor Reba." Joan shook her head.

"Men," agreed Stacey.

"Is there any particular reason you are accosting me in the hallway," he asked, noting the elevator still hadn't arrived and the stairwell sat at the opposite end, meaning he'd have to shove through a great many women. Not exactly something he wanted to attempt.

"Just asking some questions. Do you have a problem with questions?" Melly's turn to press in close and glare at him. She wore dark-rimmed glasses that magnified her glare.

"To answer a question, shouldn't you ask

one?"

"What are you doing with Reba?" Luna might lack height, but she made up for it in attitude.

"I thought we ascertained I did Reba." He couldn't help a hint of a smile, and it didn't waver as a very tall lioness stared him in the eye.

"I didn't hear any screaming. Does that mean you suck in the sack?"

The shorter Melly tapped her chin contemplatively. "Maybe he gagged her. You know, with his equipment."

Too many eyes suddenly veered their stare low, under-the-belt low, and a less brash man might have shriveled under their combined stare. "We are not discussing my genitalia."

"Genitalia?" Luna chuckled. "That is the prissiest thing I've ever heard."

"What a way to ruin a cock," grumbled Stacey. "Even manhood or shaft is preferable. You might as well have used the P word."

"Penis?"

"Pencil dick. No girl ever wants to hear that." Nods all around.

Nuts. They truly were nuts, and they said zombies were hard to reason with. "Are you always this crass so early in the morning?" he asked.

"Only when inspired," Stacey replied.

It occurred to him in that moment that he knew too much of the local lion pride if he knew them all by face and name. Since when had he gotten involved with the local menagerie?

Since he'd met a kitten who made him want to stroke until she purred. "If you don't mind, I have business to attend."

"What kind of business?" Luna's eyes narrowed in suspicion.

A finger jabbed. "And why isn't Reba going with you?"

"She's sleeping off the effects of her extreme…" He paused to give them a slow grin, and a hot push of electrified air. "*Pleasure.*"

"Oooh." Their eyes widened.

Ding. The door behind him opened, and he stepped in, facing forward and watching the women. They formed a half circle around the opening, their amber lion gazes watching him, wary, but not threatening. He hit the button for the lobby. It should have required a fingerprint swipe or a keycard at the very least. A building like this kept its people secure. Gaston needed nothing but a simple touch to get where he wanted. Magic always seemed to stymy science, and he used that to this advantage.

But Gaston had finally found something that stymied him. Reba. When he'd met her, he'd felt an instant attraction. A fascination with her boldness, her confident nature. His interest in her should have waned by now. He should have been able to easily set her aside, and yet, he found he couldn't. The more time they spent together, the more times he met his fantasy version on the dreamscape, the more deeply he found himself falling, and he recognized that frightening feeling.

Falling in love? Not again. The last time hadn't ended well. Hadn't ended at all, given he kept having to deal with his first false love over and over and over again.

However, was it right to paint love with the tarnished brush of his experience? Should he avoid affection for another simply because a past experience jaded him?

Until now, that was exactly what he'd done. He'd forsaken love. Don't mistake him; he had paramours. He'd slept with women on every continent, in every city. Some might label him a rake, but he preferred to see himself as a man of vast experience. Yet, over the past few years, how many women had he taken to bed? Few, so few, and none that intrigued him past a meeting or two. They bored him. He couldn't maintain an interest. Until Reba.

Reba fascinated him. Drew him. She made him want things he thought he'd never want again.

A life. Home. A family...

It was easy to ignore these frightening feelings when she refused his advances. Easy to pretend she didn't exist when he never saw her. Before he touched her...

However, now he had touched her and tasted her and, as a result, wanted her more than ever. Perhaps he could have still walked away, but she just had to tell him she wanted to claim him. This woman who embodied perfection wanted him on her terms.

Wanted.

Him.

Fuck. He'd deal with it later. He needed to get his head in the game and deal with what happened now. The shitstorm erupting around him.

He made it to his vehicle without further interruption and drove out of the underground parking garage. Not yet dawn, the city streets were quiet; a Saturday morning wasn't exactly prime time for traffic. He opted to keep the radio off, enjoying the simplicity of silence. Underrated if you asked him. There was so much noise nowadays. Everywhere, noise.

Even with the radio and television off, things hummed, the refrigerator, the cooling/heating system. And even if you escaped those modern conveniences to a room with no vents or appliances, you still heard the electricity humming in the wires. Very distracting.

A man raised in a simpler time and place, he often chose the quiet, which was why his interest in Reba and her vivid conversation surprised him.

The light before him switched to red, and he slowed his car, tapping his fingers on the wheel. As soon as he left the condo, he'd texted JF to meet him at the club. He needed to assess the damage and file a report with his insurance. Then there would be no avoiding meeting with the police again. They'd surely want to—

Crash. The impact from behind tossed his car into the intersection, in time for it to get slammed by a car coming the other way.

"Fuck me!" he yelled, trying to brace himself, but unable as his body whiplashed.

Metal screamed as it twisted and tore. Glass shattered. The air bags deployed, saving him from the worst of the damage, but that didn't unpin him from his car. He was trapped in it, his leg pinned by the steering column. The doors jammed shut from the torsion of the frame.

The drivers that hit him staggered from their cars, one of them moaning, "OhmygodwhatdidIdo?"

Through the side window, honeycombed with cracks, he could have sworn he saw blonde hair. The woman turned and smiled. Vivienne raised a hand

and waved then blew him a kiss.

I am going to wring your neck! But he was stuck. Stuck in his car for hours as emergency crews were called, and organized chaos ensued as they secured the scene, cleaned up the gasoline spill, and waited for the arrivals of the jaws of life to extract him.

Because some things even magic couldn't do. At least not in public. And worst of all, his phone died mid text.

Fuck!

He knew Vivienne somehow machinated the accident, but obviously she didn't want to kill him. Not yet. She liked to play games. This game smelled of delay. She wanted to slow him down. To put her players into place. Without a phone, he couldn't do the same, not stuck as he was. And once he escaped the police with their questions, then the paramedics, he had to work fast. Real fast because a certain drug would wear off.

The sleeping lioness would wake. And she wouldn't be happy.

Chapter Fourteen

Waking up to Stacey hovering face upside down above her was bad enough. The dangling plastic spider—which resulted in Reba screaming and batting at it before grabbing the baseball bat by the bed and trying to whack it into oblivion then chasing Stacey around the bedroom to whack her—might have put her in a bit of a bad mood. Remembering Tony had drugged her and taken off without her put Reba in a really foul one.

"I can't believe he did that to me." It wasn't just the abandonment and drugging that pissed her off. Those were pretty bad, but knowing she'd been comatose for at least eight hours frightened. Anything could have happened—shaved eyebrows, permanent marker mustache, Instagram pictures showing her slobbering in her sleep. "That prick! What if aliens arrived and wanted to conduct anal probes on me? How would I have protected myself?" Don't laugh. It had happened. Just ask her Aunt Betunia.

"Oh, he made sure you had protection. He texted us after he left. Told the biatches to keep an eye on you."

He did? That was kind of sweet. Maybe she wouldn't prolong his death. "So you've been here this entire time?"

"Some of it. Meena was here too, with Leo.

147

Word is they got a little frisky. You might want to have someone clean the couch, and the rug."

Burning was more foolproof.

"And Melly popped in. She might have borrowed a few things from your closet."

Melly might burn, too, if she didn't return them.

"Where is he?" *Where oh where did my dead boyfriend go?*

"Do I look like his fucking secretary?" Stacey rolled her eyes. "He texted and said he was on his way to some meetings and that you needed your sleep but he was having a problem with some crazy broad who tends to go after his girlfriends and so would we mind looking after your skanky ass."

"He told you that? You know what that means, right?"

Stacey grinned. "He called you his girlfriend."

The high-five was vigorous. "Okay, so my idiot boyfriend"—cue the giggle—"thinks he can just run off and deal with a psychotic sorceress who can call upon the minions of Hell."

"Back the fuck up. No way. You're making it up."

"I am being totally serious here. You're looking at a demon killer. I already fought some of the little bastards, which taste bad, by the way. Bring plenty of mouthwash."

"What about the part where a psychotic witch is their master?"

"His ex is having separation issues. Looks like she's behind a lot of the shit happening around town, including the mutiny issue with those wanker guys that work for Tony."

"Wanker." Stacey snickered. "I'll bet they like that nickname."

"Maybe they'd care if there were some left. There aren't many, like three I think." Much like the pride, Tony didn't put up with shit, even from his own crew. When you lived in hiding from the human race, you couldn't take chances with your secrets. "The rest of his staff is mostly human, plus a few unaligned shifters working the club."

"So is it true his special dudes are vampire gargoyles?" Stacey mentioned.

"Kind of and not. They're not made of rock, but they do drink blood. They're also total downers. I swear that Jean Francois is such a snob. Makes me want to wedgie him."

"Sounds like the demons are more fun."

"They are." Reba clapped her hands. "And Tony says there will be more because this Vivienne chick is a total magic hack. We're going to probably have to fight all kinds of messed-up dudes."

"You know what this means?" Stacey's eyes brightened.

"Yes I do." Reba's smile slowly curled. "It means we're about to battle to save our city and pride from the forces of evil."

"We're going to be heroes, which means…"

"…we're going to need outfits!" And not just any outfit would do.

As Reba spent that day shopping, having to use a detour route to the mall because of some major accident nearby, she wondered what Tony was doing. She'd fired him a few texts. Gotten no reply.

Playing hard to get. Adorable.

She fired a few more texts to Tony's second,

Jean Francois. He at least replied. His last one back? *I don't know who let the dog out*. Still made her giggle.

Word of the accident involving her boyfriend eventually trickled to her, but since Tony apparently had walked away, she spent her time worrying about other things. Such as, would eating that second brownie mean she'd have to have a third? Hmm, perhaps she should play it safe and have four. She also stashed a pair in her purse for later.

At one point, she and the gaggle of women hanging out at Stacey's place, going wild with the sewing machine, got a dossier on the very naughty Vivienne. A slim file because the bitch knew how to hide her tracks.

A wily foe. Fun times. Meow.

The ladies of the pride went over the details of Vivienne's file, arguing some of its points.

"Anyone else notice this ho has been twenty-nine years old for an awful long time?" Stacey made a moue of annoyance, probably because she was still pissed they'd lit thirty sparklers in her condo and set off the sprinklers. The insurance had replaced most of the stuff. They'd learned their lesson after doing it in a car. Who knew distracted driving would have such a big fine?

Luna layered some of the stuff they'd printed on the floor, most of it newspaper articles gleaned from the Internet. Amazing what facial recognition software and technology could do.

Melly, their resident hack, had managed to grab copies of the surveillance footage from Tony's apartment building and, when those showed no one using Tony's elevator other than Reba, went to street cams next until they spotted Vivienne, there one minute under a lamppost, gone the next.

"How did she get from here"—Luna stabbed the grainy black and white picture—"to here?" She jabbed at the color image taken the previous night by a witness to the flames shooting from the windows of Gaston's place. "And I'm going to assume she got out again." All without getting caught on the building's cameras.

"I'm going with invisibility cloak. I call dibs on it!" Meena's hand shot up.

"She does not have an invisibility cloak." Although, if she did, Reba wanted it. "And it's a neat trick, except I saw Tony do it first."

"Did your Tony make it to a penthouse suite without using stairs or an elevator?" Luna pointed to the elevator logs. "We see you on the camera, first arriving, then leaving. But we don't see it moving at all for hours before and not at all after you left."

"She could have tampered with the logs," Joan remarked, pausing in her making of some kind of power drink that involved too many green leafy things. Blech.

"Hacking is one possibility. I got in pretty easy," Melly remarked.

"I think she used magic and like teleported." Stacey whirled, her red tresses, so unusual for a lioness, trailing behind her.

"I think you need to stop sniffing the catnip."

The whirling stopped as Stacey glared at Luna. "I wouldn't have to sniff it if someone hadn't gotten into trouble the last time Cook made us some brownies."

"It wasn't the brownies that made me take a nap in the park. That patch of grass was soft and warm." And Luna couldn't resist it. The girl liked to sunbathe—naked.

"If we're done missing the good ol' days of catnip candies"—also known as their wild college years, which cost the pride a fortune in cover-ups—"can we concentrate on the bitch who's after my boyfriend?" Snicker. Still wasn't getting old.

"I might have lucked out," Melly announced, tapping away on her laptop excitedly. "That witch broad is good at hiding, especially since she seems to pay cash and not leave a paper trail. But in order to rent a certain building downtown, she had to provide identification. Even better, we own that building." The pride owned many assets in the city. "Which means we've got access as her landlords."

Reba wasn't the only one to look down at her outfit and make a moue of disappointment. "But what if I don't want to change and be business like?"

Meena stood and planted her hands on her hips. Impressive hips. Child-bearing hips according to Dmitri, who'd married her twin. "I'll make the sacrifice and go. I even have a suit. Leo made me buy it so I'd look respectable."

Once they stopped laughing, Meena guffawing hardest of all, they got back to business.

"Leo will kick your ass if you go in there seeing as how you're with child. *His* child," said with emphasis. Luna rolled her eyes. They all did. You'd think the pride Omega was the first man to ever impregnate a woman.

"Shhh. Don't speak his name." Meena bit her lip and peeked at the front door. "He'll know we're plotting and make me take some vitamins."

More than one person bit her lip so as to not

snicker.

"I'll go in the front," Luna volunteered. "Melly will stick close by in our surveillance van helping us with the computers and cameras." Luna tossed out assignments like Frisbees. People often thought the lionesses of the pride were a mob without rule. They just didn't understand organized chaos. "Joan, Stacey, Reba, and I will enter from here, here, and here." Luna pointed out the various points of egress, from the back loading door to the sewer—Joan drew the short piece of yarn on that one—to the rooftop, and, finally, the employee parking garage.

"We taking any of the boys with us?" Meena asked, Luna relenting enough to let her sit in the van to guard Melly. "Leo's always saying I get into trouble without him."

"He's just jealous at all the fun you have," Luna remarked. "Jeoff is the same way. And he cramps my style. Always trying to protect me." She rolled her eyes. "So cute. But for this one, we're going to be on our own. They're already dealing with some other issues around town. Man stuff according to Arik." Luna uttered a scornful sound.

"From what I hear, the stuff they're checking out is probably related to this Viv character and those ghoul things Reba saw." Stacey volunteered the information.

"The sooner we take down this heifer, the sooner we can rub it in their faces that we're more awesome. Ready?"

"Does a lion pee on the carpet?"

Hands slapped down, one on top of the other, hard and brisk. They also uttered their team shout.

"Baddest Biatches. Meow!"

Don't worry, Tony, I'm gonna help save the day. Then she was going to slap him silly for being such a moron. Going off to save the world without her. She might give him two slaps for that. Then she'd kiss him better.

Chapter Fifteen

"Sugar, what a surprise finding you here." Exclaimed by a much-too-familiar female voice.

A part of Gaston wasn't truly surprised to turn around and see Reba on the rooftop, although her outfit did make his eyes widen. She wore a hot pink bodysuit with a utility belt and a short white cape that matched her knee-high go-go boots. A white fabric mask covered the top half of her face, the edges of it glittering with small crystals.

"Dare I ask what you're wearing?"

She placed a hand on her hip and posed. "Do you like it? We had them emblazoned this afternoon."

He liked it very much. It would look even better on the floor. "What's it supposed to mean?"

"For the moment, it's supposed to signify Baddest Biatches, but Ellony, who's our marketing manager, says that might not work with the television networks and their stupid censors. But she says my superhero name should be fine."

"Superhero name?"

She grinned. "I'm Pounce, on account I—"

"Stop the insanity right there. You are not a superhero."

"Well of course I'm not, not yet. Vivienne is still at large. I need to vanquish her first."

The convoluted logic made a strange sense.

"Except you're not going to be vanquishing anyone. My staff and I will handle this."

"You don't have enough minions to do shit."

True, his numbers were less than ideal. However, this wasn't the eighteenth century with primitive magic and weapons.

"I have been fighting Vivienne fine up until now."

"How about we end this thing instead?"

He would like nothing better. Gaston had spent his day after getting yanked from the debris of his car answering questions. *"Who's got a grudge against you?", "Are you involved in criminal activity?"* As if he had time for the petty questions of humans and shifters. It took a bit of magic, and a lot of patience, before he managed to leave all the questions behind and get a message to JF. His second swung by to grab him—and lecture Gaston.

"She is really irritating me this time." As per usual, Vivienne never attacked him directly. She went at him sideways, with fires and accidents and subversion. She never did anything to strike at him directly. Probably because she feared if he got too close he'd strangle her with his bare hands.

"Perhaps, instead of chasing after her from city to city, you should just leave her alone," Jean Francois said as he pulled out into traffic. "This only started again because you keep hunting her down."

"She needs to pay."

"Hasn't she paid enough?"

For killing his sister, his only family, and then compounding that atrocity?

"She murdered my sister." Of course, he might have started that particular series of events.

When Gaston found out his fiancée was cheating, he kind of set her house on fire. It killed her cat, who, as it turned out, was more than a household feline. He'd destroyed her familiar. The retaliation proved fierce.

"She might have killed Celine, but since then, you have taken away everything she ever loved."

True. Revenge was all he had after his sibling died, came back, and then died again—by his hand—before Celine could start an undead revolution. If only he'd known then the things he did now. Perhaps he could have saved his sister like he saved JF and the others, turning them into whampyrs that they might evade death.

But that was a secret he learned too late.

He'd vowed to never be too late again. To never let Vivienne get too comfortable. To never let her rest. He always hunted her, and for the first time in a very long time, the stakes were high. High because he now had someone he cared about, and she was on the rooftop with him, acting like this was some kind of game.

Another man might have turned angry and yelled at her to leave. A lesser man would plead. He attempted logic. "You shouldn't have come. I left you behind for a reason."

"Thanks for making sure I got my beauty rest. Best sleep I've had in ages." She stretched, which drew his eye to places that distracted him from his purpose.

"I did it to keep you out of danger."

"But I like danger. Why do you think I like you so much?"

She liked him? The blatant admission took him by surprise, so he wasn't prepared for the arms she flung around his neck.

"You should leave. Now." He tried to use his best stern voice.

Judging by the nip of his chin by her sharp white teeth, she didn't respect it at all. "Not happening. I'm staying right here and helping you. Even if I'm still mad at you."

"You're mad at me? For what?" Everything he'd done was for her own good. *She should thank me.* Instead, she chided.

"Drugging a woman is a felony in all the states. But don't worry. I'm not going to kill you for doing it. I am, however, really looking forward to the angry sex followed by makeup sex."

Angry sex? As if he could remain angry with her. He wrapped an arm around her waist and drew her close. While he wouldn't admit it to Reba, he had the utmost respect for the fact that she wanted to be by his side. She didn't lack for courage, and he already knew she was fierce in a fight.

"If I let you come with me, promise you'll obey."

"You're going to give me orders? That is so *hot.*"

"*Chaton.*" He growled the endearment. "Behave."

"Or else what?" she asked, all sassy impertinence.

He spun her in his grasp until her backside fitted against his groin, and his hands stroked down the spandex fabric of her suit, skimming over the lines of her body, leaving her trembling. She always reacted so intensely to his touch, just like he couldn't help his own attraction to her.

The exploring hand reached her mound and cupped it. The heat of her filled his palm. He rubbed, and she let out a sound, a guttural moan. His lips pressed against the pulse on her neck. "Be good or you won't get any more of this." Squeeze.

"Sugar, that has got to be the biggest steak anyone has ever dangled in front of me. I'll be good. But can we hurry things along? My girly parts need attention in a bad way, which is rather distracting."

He knew all about distraction. He held it in his arms. "I'm waiting for a signal from JF. He's going to let me know when Vivienne enters the building."

"Does that mean we have a little bit of time? Awesome." She pulled away from him and stepped to the parapet, which was slightly more than a leap to the next building, the one they were targeting.

"What are you doing?"

"Today you witness history as you see a cat fly." Less fly and more like zip lined across as she pressed something on her belt that shot out and latched onto the chimney the next building over. Apparently, she didn't pause to think what would happen once it did affix itself and began reeling the line back in. With a squealed, "Whee!" Reba went flying off the building, arms and legs akimbo, not at all perturbed that she would probably smash face-first into the solid side.

Time to be a hero again. She certainly kept him busy. "Dammit." Gaston hopped onto the ledge and jumped, his black cloak more than a warm covering. It billowed behind him, very much in the style of a certain dark hero, but his didn't rely on science.

"*Levati.*" The word of power imbued him with a short-term ability to stay aloft, and so he managed a graceful glide and planned to scoop Reba on the way, except he apparently didn't give her enough credit.

She flipped in mid-air and grabbed hold of the thin rope reeling her in. She hit the other building feet first and then rappelled upward the rest of the way. He beat her there, but not by much. A moment before landing, he whispered another word of power, "*Celaverimi.*" Conceal, because now the game truly began.

Reba ran over the top of the rooftop ledge and quickly flicked her grappling hook so that it slid back within the belt.

"Cool toy," he observed.

"Thanks. Melly designed it. She's a total techno geek."

"What other surprises do you have inside your belt?"

"You'll have to strip it off me to see." She winked, and the temptation to find out now almost had him grabbing her.

"Later." No time for naughty pleasures. Despite his concealing magic, their arrival didn't go unnoticed. A bright red light illuminated above a camera as it activated.

Reba waved.

"What are you doing?"

"Don't worry. Melly's got it. As far as anyone inside can see, the rooftop is clear."

Of course it was clear, because he'd also screwed with the observation electronics—but his was more of a cloaking maneuver, which proved taxing, especially given the area he tried to cover. So he took Reba at her word, assumed Melly had the cameras locked down, and released the spell.

"I'm surprised there are no guards up here," she noted, pirouetting around, the back of her suit barely hugging her rounded cheeks. "I don't see anything interesting."

"Then you're not looking in the right places." His attention diverted from the perfect splendor of her body as he spotted movement. A twitch of a hard surface as one of the stubby chimneys came to life, the metal golem blending in well with the other rooftop items. The magic animating it barely discernible, the weaving of it very subtle. Earth magic always appeared low key. It was also a solid magic, if stupid. Golems were known for being strong and virtually impossible to stop, but dumb. So very dumb.

While the golem had some semblance of human form, two arms and legs and a head, that was where the similarities stopped. It had no hands, no fingers, no feet. It clunked on thick trunks and waved around club-like appendages. Its single gaping eye, a hole in its blockhead radiating red light, scanned the area with laser-ish intensity. Once it spotted a target, it went after it with single-minded purpose—destroy.

Knowing what he faced, Gaston's plan was simple. Coax the creature toward him and send it soaring down over the edge, a several story fall that would pulverize it.

A great plan, if he were alone. Reba, however, felt a need to do things her way. And her way was very naked.

"What are you doing?" he asked, turning his attention from the lumbering golem as skin flashed from the corner of his eye.

"Don't worry, sugar. My lioness will save your sweet ass." Sure enough, Reba changed, cocoa skin morphing into sleek dark fur. She might not sport a mane like a male lion, but her lithe shape was plenty impressive and sleek. It also was no good against the golem.

Claws gripping the roof's asphalt surface, she ran at the metal creature, leaped, and hit it.

Clang. She bounced back and hit the ground less than gracefully. She sat up and shook her head. Undaunted, she tried again, slashing at the golem with claws that resulted in an awful sound, nails on chalkboard times a thousand. Everyone in a several mile radius probably winced.

Next, she tried to bite and hardly left a dent.

"Allow me, *chaton*." Gaston put himself between the golem and Reba. Vivienne could be so predictable. Having expected this type of monster, he knew just what to do.

A flick of his wrist and a dust appeared in the air. He blew the particles at the golem. The powder hit, and rust spots appeared on the creature, harmless to humans, but the corrosive stuff only had to hit metal to start eating. The creaking and groaning of metal joints grew in volume as the golem staggered after Gaston. He ducked and dodged the massive clubs it had for arms.

The golem never noticed the edge of the building as it chased after Gaston. Reba, having caught on to his plan, lunged her feline form at the metal creation and gave it the shove in the ass needed to topple it over. She peeked over the edge as it hit the ground and smashed onto the hood of a car.

She turned her head and cocked it, as if asking, *"Think anyone will notice?"*

"There won't be any hiding that," he observed. "We should get inside before the building is locked down."

He scooped her clothes—barely a handful of fabric, the belt heavier than it looked—and she followed as he led the way inside, the electronic lock giving way before him.

Once inside the building, he immediately took point and went down the stairs until he reached a door. A door without runes. A door without a guard.

Not even a keypad. It seemed too easy. He noted the camera in the corner of the stairwell, the one concession to security. Did Melly of the pride still control it? Or did Vivienne watch them right now?

He pulled back his sleeve and tapped at the screen for his watch. A prototype more powerful than any smartphone. His second hadn't texted him to say Vivienne arrived. That didn't mean she hadn't. She knew how to apparate just about anywhere without notice. A mistress when it came to sleight of mind.

Was she here, though?

He eyed the closed door. Battered gray metal and a pewter-hued handle. No window. What lay on the other side? Were they even in the right place?

He resorted to old-fashioned methods and pressed his ear against the portal. The cool, hard surface held a slight hum, that of a building live with energy. Beyond that, though? Quiet, so very quiet, which was why her whispered, "Hear anything?" sounded so fucking loud.

Gaston didn't think, he reacted, flipping her to the wall beside the door, his lips mashing against hers demanding silence. At least that was how it started, but as usual when he touched her, lust overtook common sense. One kiss turned into a never-ending embrace. Lips sliding over lips. Tongues dancing with sensual abandon.

It only made him crave more. More of her. His hand skimmed down her frame, tracing his way to her thighs. She'd not had time to dress in between shifting, which meant he stroked skin. Soft skin. And thighs, sweet thighs that parted at his touch. His fingers slid between and stroked across her cleft.

"Why is it you're always wet when I touch you?" he murmured softly against her lips.

"Because I want you." Her hips thrust against his hand.

How he wanted her too, with such desperation, but now wasn't the time for sex.

Apparently, it was his turn to speak out loud. "When will there be a time?" she murmured.

"The loss of the golem won't go unnoticed. An alarm will have sounded."

"So we've got limited time?" The idea seemed to please rather than dismay her.

"Very limited, as in someone could come through that door or up those stairs at any moment."

"Way to sell it. We'd better be quick," she growled. She tugged at his belt. "I can't stand it anymore."

Madness. Pure madness. He should stop her. He didn't joke when he'd said they could be discovered at any moment. Someone could barge through that door, locked and loaded...and he just didn't fucking care.

She was right. When would there be time? Time was wherever they chose to take it. *We need to make time.*

No matter the danger.

Boner. And he wasn't ashamed of it. Only someone who'd never truly experienced the adrenaline that came of having to do something wrong, yet pleasurable, could understand. The thrill of discovery almost counted as an orgasm.

She asked for quick. He could do quick. When she released his cock from his pants, he wasted no time and hoisted her, hands on her waist, her back pinned against the wall. Without him asking, her legs came around his waist, his cloak hiding them from sight. At least they wouldn't be seen by those on camera, and even better, it did not impede at all the exquisite sensation of sliding into her.

The head of his cock penetrated the slick opening of her sex with ease. She was so damned tight and hot and wet and perfect. He pushed into her, harder and thicker than he'd ever recalled. Every see-saw of motion stuttered his breath and jolted him with pleasure.

In. Hissing breath in.

Out. A low groan and then a gasp from her as he slammed back in.

In. Out. A decadent and tortuous thrust into his woman. *My woman.* His. And he could claim her right now.

Too fast? He wanted to hold back, to hold on to this moment, but urgency drove him. Not just an urgency that had to do with time or getting caught, but a simple urgency to place his mark on this woman. *To make her mine.*

"Yes, yours," she whispered as if in reply.

It spurred him on faster. He slammed his dick home, deep inside her, and she clawed at his shoulders, the tips of her fingers digging through fabric. Her lips clung to his, and her breath turned ragged, as ragged as his own as he thrust into her, no finesse, no leisure, no technique. Just raw, unbridled passion. And she loved it.

Little mewls of pleasure escaped her, and her digging fingers grew sharp and pricked him, tearing at his shirt, even scratching at his skin. Her mouth left his to suck at his neck, and he arched his head back, pounding into her, already on the brink of pleasure. Forget holding back. He was done holding back.

Her channel clenched around him, one tight squeeze, and then she came, came so hard, and yet, she didn't cry out. She bit him instead, clamped her teeth on his neck, and damn it all, she broke skin. But he didn't care; the sharp pain had him coming. Coming so fucking hard, and when she growled, "Mine," he couldn't help but agree.

"So fucking mine." *Mine. Mine. Mine.*

The word echoed with joyful abandon and felt so right. So damned right for the first time in a long time.

The moment proved fucking perfect.

Which was why he was so pissed when someone opened the door beside them and gagged quite loudly.

Chapter Sixteen

"Go away." Tony growled, tucking his cloak tight around them while, at the same time, attempting to put away his dangly bits. The dear man was shy. Adorable, especially given his club catered to the more hedonistic lifestyle. Did Tony prefer watching to being watched?

"I will not go away. And you'd better be getting dressed. This is not the time for that kind of stuff." Luna sounded quite peeved and proper. What was up with her chastising them on public indecency?

Very suspicious. Luna never told anyone to get their clothes on. Hell, she'd been known to get naked at the oddest times, sometimes in public.

Was something wrong with Luna? Reba eyed her friend, dressed as she recalled, but looking a hell of a lot more pissed than usual.

"What yanked your tail?" Reba asked. "Are you getting pissy because you didn't bring Jeoff along for a little hanky-panky?"

"This isn't the time for hanky-panky."

"There's always time. Is this what mating does to you?" Reba shook her head. "And to think I looked up to you as the cool one."

"I'm cool." Reba offered her a placating smile, and Luna's scowl deepened. "We don't have time for this. The place is empty. As in we showed up to party and no one was home."

"Are you sure about that? We saw a golem thing on the roof. Could be there's more hidden dudes hanging around." Her nose twitched and twitched at the smell on this level. Something burned and made it hard to properly scent.

"Oh we found a few foes. One demon and a report of some ghouls in the basement. No biggie. Nothing to see." Luna dropped her gaze to a place below Tony's waist.

That more than anything flustered him. So cute.

"I highly doubt the building is empty. You probably just can't see the threat." Regaining some of his cool factor, Tony crossed his arms, his body a barrier in front of Reba as she struggled into her suit. Her awesome superhero outfit had twisted and rolled on itself and refused to cooperate. When she did manage to slip it on, it rubbed over the sensitized areas of her body. It made her shiver in pleasure, and remembrance.

The man knew how to play her body. Meow.

And I claimed him. Bigger meow. Of course, she was going to wait until later to mention that part to her sugar. Given his usual reaction to stuff, she expected him to flip. She wanted a bed nearby when that happened because the sex would be epic when they made up—that and she wanted to avoid rug burn.

"You seem to give Vivienne much credit," Luna said, her eyes narrowed and appraising him.

"She's a worthy opponent. I've learned to not underestimate."

"Well then you shouldn't be surprised this building is a decoy. We're in the wrong spot."

Reba popped her head around Tony's arm and frowned in Luna's direction. "Melly was wrong? Did hell freeze over?"

"We were outsmarted. Apparently, the action is happening on the far side of town. There are reports of bodies, and they look like they've been mauled. Twitter feeds are also exploding with claims they're hearing gunshots. And there's even a mention of zombie-like fellows."

"We missed out on a ghoul attack? Bummer. All we got was a golem." Reba faked a pout because, really, her girly parts were much too happy still to feel disappointment.

"If Vivienne is moving so publicly, then we need to prepare so that we are ready. I should speak to JF." Pulling out his phone, Tony held it up and frowned, probably on account some of these buildings had shitty cell service. He moved away, down the wide hall, a space lined with only a few closed doors. Tony chose one at random and disappeared from sight.

The closed doors fascinated, especially since the plaques held such high-brow titles like CEO and President. Anyone inside? The nearest door gave at her touch and she peeked in, a square room with a desk chair and a small-seated reception area. Empty of people. A very closed-in room, especially since the dim recessed lighting and a lack of windows spelled a gloomy ambiance.

Ugh. No sun. That would depress her if she had to deal with that every day.

Reba pressed on to the inner sanctum door, and it also gave at her touch. It opened onto a more lavish space with floor-to-ceiling windows, a shining hardwood floor, and a big desk. Nothing marred the surface, not a monitor or a single pen. The smell of burning incense persisted. She lifted her head to the vents.

Sniff. "What's that stuff that is pumping through the vents?"

Luna shrugged. "Who knows. The building reeks of it."

Reba would have to trust it wouldn't kill her or drop her into a deep sleep because there was no avoiding breathing it. She was pretty sure she still had a few lives left if it proved dangerous. Of more concern was Tony. Would the stuff harm him? He'd obviously smelled it and yet didn't remark on it.

It's screwing with my nose. A part of her felt bereft without this skill she counted on. How could a girl hunt properly if she couldn't smell a thing?

She didn't like it. It smacked of a trap to her. Reba whirled from the view outside and noted Luna behind her, closer than expected. "Are we sure this place is a decoy? Melly is never wrong."

"Something spooked the sorceress. She was on her way here, even stepped out of her car—you should see her wheels, a beautiful white Rolls Royce, with a driver and everything. She steps out, and next thing we know, there's a sudden wall of fog that lasts only seconds. But enough to see she's disappeared and the car takes off. Next thing we heard, stuff was exploding on the far side of town by the docks."

Fireworks? Sounded like fun. "What are we waiting for? Let's go."

"There's not much point in rushing over. By the time we make it across town, it will be over." Luna's logic deflated.

"The girls will be kind of bummed about that. I know they were hoping for some action."

"I'm sure we're not done with Vivienne yet."

"I hope not. I'd love to say a few things to that heifer."

"Such as?"

Before Reba could launch into a list, they ran back into Tony in the hall, wearing his serious face.

"Jean Francois has confirmed. Vivienne isn't here. This entire evening was a waste."

"Is that the word you really want to use?" Reba asked, planting a hand on her hip and giving him the evil eye.

His expression softened. "Perhaps not a complete waste. Parts of it were most enjoyable; however, the primary objective of this evening has failed. If the reports are to be believed, Vivienne has more forces marshaled than expected. I need to meet with Jean Francois and plan our next course of action."

"You're going to dump me for your manservant?"

"Not dump. I will see you home first, of course."

"There is no of course here. First off, I don't need a bodyguard. And second, I'm not going home yet. The night is young. I'm still feeling frisky." Wink. "But since you'd prefer to run along and play with your lackey, then go. I've got my girls here to keep me company."

For a moment, his gaze strayed to Luna in her dull gray bodysuit emblazoned with an S, because the bitch loved to snarl, especially if you touched the last piece of bacon. "Even if Vivienne is not present, there are probably some surprises in the building. You should all leave this place before you play with something you can't handle."

"If we find a monster, we'll take care of it." Luna rolled her eyes. "We are women, not morons."

"But it is your first time dealing with creatures such as golems and ghouls and demons. Some of them can be quite treacherous if you don't know what to watch for."

"We did not survive this long being stupid." Reba couldn't help but feel stung. The man acted as if he was a chastising father instead of her lover. "I don't need you to tell me what I can and can't do." Her life, her choices, even the bad ones.

"As if you'd listen," he grumbled. "Fine. Have it your way. But if something should happen to you"—he glared down at her—"then you can expect me—"

"To say I told you so. Yada yada. Whatever." Reba couldn't help a roll of her eyes.

"Actually, my impetuous kitten, I was going to say if anything happens to you, then my vengeance won't be pretty. I won't let anyone harm you. *Ever.*" The panty-wetting words went with an even more lust-inducing kiss, the hotness of it stealing all breath and igniting a firestorm between them.

Dear God. Would it always be this way? She wrapped herself around him as much as she could, and even Luna's gagging noises couldn't stop her from thoroughly enjoying it.

He set her down. Slowly. He tilted her chin and said softly, "Be safe, *chaton.*" Then he was gone, a quick stride taking him down the hall, his black cloak whipping behind him. So fucking hot. She watched her hot sugar until he got on the elevator and it left. She counted to five and then turned to a very quiet Luna.

"So, now that we've gotten rid of my boyfriend like you wanted, what's the real scoop?" Reba asked. She flexed her fingers, readying the nails.

"What makes you think I lied?" Luna batted her lashes with the most ridiculous attempt at innocence.

"Did you really think you'd fool me? The scent thing was a good decoy, but I know you're not Luna. What have you done to my friend?"

"Nothing, but…" The image before Reba wavered. "I can't say the same thing for you." Luna disappeared, and Vivienne appeared, in all her cute blonde glory, and Reba couldn't help but shake her head.

"Damn, you're good. How the hell did you mimic Luna so well?" Duplicated right down to the outfit and sneer. There was just one thing Viv couldn't replicate, and that was the inner lion. And Reba's feline immediately noticed. It took Reba herself to listen to the words spoken to realize there was a lack of profanity in the conversation.

"Taking on the appearance of someone else only takes a single strand of hair and the right spell. It's usually undetectable. But you say you knew. If true, why didn't you tell Gaston?"

"Because he's too nice to have to deal with you."

"Too nice?" The words emerged in a high-pitched screech. "The man is a murderous bastard. He has been following me around for decades, destroying my homes, laying waste to my resources."

"And yet you're still alive and calling him fiancé."

"Because he is still mine." A jealous green glow lit Viv's gaze. "He might dally with you, but he is mine."

"Think again. And just so you know, while he might have held back from killing you, I won't. Lions might play, but we always get our prey."

"You want to fight me?" Viv's head cocked, and her blonde hair jiggled as if alive. "How fascinating. Smart people run. Or stand there and piss themselves. Wreaks havoc on hardwoods, you know. The smell never quite comes out."

"Are you supposed to be scary?" Reba eyed the diminutive female. "I'm just not seeing it." There were no monsters at her back, and she wore no jewelry, so no hidden powders like Tony enjoyed employing.

"You think I am weaker than you." The harmonious giggle only reinforced her non-villainous persona. "You are wrong. So wrong. And stupid too. You should have told Gaston while you had a chance. He's the only one who's ever come close to besting me." Viv twitched her fingers, and Reba's eyes widened as invisible bands wrapped around her. Squeezing tight enough her ribs protested.

"What are you doing? I thought you wanted to fight."

"Fight yes, fight fair?" A sly smile pulled Viv's lips as she shook her head. "Isn't all fair in love and war? And make no mistake, this is war. I know Gaston has feelings for you. Naughty man. Trying to make me jealous. It worked. I am positively green-eyed."

For some reason Reba couldn't help but think in a certain wise green creature's voice, *The delusion is strong in this one. Show her the way, I must.* "Tony hates you."

The slender hand waved the claim away. "He's a little angry still with me over a mistake made a long time ago. I might have killed someone by accident. Or on purpose. It happens. Especially when the girl saw too much. What else could I do? Your kind knows sometimes we have to kill to keep a secret. How was I to know he was so attached to the little brat? Now he thinks he hates me, but only because he still loves me." The madness in her eyes shone bright.

"Bitch, you are all kinds of crazy."

Fingers wrapped in Reba's hair, yanking her back that Viv might whisper mere inches from her ear. "Name calling will only make it hurt more. And I promise it will hurt. It has to hurt to ensure Gaston learns his lesson."

Wanna eat her.

Her lioness had a simple answer, and she was right. Reba had spent enough time talking to the girl missing a few marbles and her straightjacket. Time to flip things around. "I guess we're going to do this the hard way." Go go, lioness. Reba pulled at her feline, pulled hard, and, despite the invisible bands around her, burst free, fangs and fur and power, so much raw animal power. She lunged at Vivienne, ready to tear off her face, only it turned out Gaston wasn't the only one with sleep powder that appeared out of nowhere to hit a girl in the face.

Thump.

Chapter Seventeen

What did I miss?

As he descended in the elevator, something nagged at Gaston, but it wasn't until he hit the main lobby and saw an impossibility dressed in a gray bodysuit emblazoned with an S that his unease exploded.

There was only one way Luna had made it to this level before him.

"Fucking bitch!" And fucking brat because there was no way Reba had mistaken an imposter for her friend. *While I was too addled by the sex to think straight.* The perils of a man with a big dick and a limited blood supply.

"Excuse me? Did you just say you wanted to die?" The feisty blonde immediately went into battle mode, which, given her outfit, much like Reba's, made her look cute instead of dangerous.

"I don't suppose we just ran into each other on the top floor?"

"I have yet to get out of this level on account the elevators have been locked down. Melly has been working on them. Although, if you ask me, this place is a bust. I walked through the front doors, and there wasn't even a guard sitting behind the desk."

A decoy within a decoy. Fuck. "It was a trap." A very clever trap meant to capture someone. "We need to get up to the top floor. Vivienne has Reba."

He stepped back into the elevator and jabbed the number for the top floor.

Luna followed with an arched brow. "Don't you mean Reba has her? Don't underestimate my girl."

"I know she's a vicious fighter, among shifters and humans. But that's not what she's facing. None of you understand just how much power Vivienne can draw on. Add to that she's not quite sane and you've got—"

"A super fun time." Stacey hopped into the elevator moments before the doors shut.

"I'm surrounded by madness." He found himself strangely comforted by it. He knew he could count on these women to help him get Reba back.

"Not madness, but you are surrounded by lionesses, you poor bastard. We're much crazier." Luna winked.

"I think we might need crazy."

"Don't worry, Charlemagne. Reba will be fine."

For now. That wouldn't last. Vivienne surely had a reason for why she wanted Reba alone. It just wouldn't bode well for his kitten.

Why won't this stupid elevator hurry? The ascent seemed to take forever. At fifteen, it slowed and stopped. The doors took an eternity to slide open, and he was stepping through before they were done, eyeing the empty hall and cursing.

"They're gone." It was his fault. His fucking fault for not realizing whom he faced. Vivienne had probably taken off with Reba the moment he left.

How could I leave? How did I not realize she was an imposter? Because he'd let his dick think for him. His lack of common sense cost him dearly. A lump at the end of the hall drew his attention. It was his kitten's belt, fallen to the floor. He shoved through the door, breath held past the spot he'd so recently claimed her, and climbed the set of stairs to the roof. He arrived too late, the fading beat of helicopter rotors a mocking reminder of his failure.

A heap of fabric on the tarred asphalt was all that remained. He sank to his knees and clasped the bodysuit to his chest. Reba had obviously shifted but hadn't prevailed. *And I was too late.*

He staggered back down the stairs and, upon seeing the lionesses, snapped, "They're gone." His words didn't stop Luna and Stacey with grim faces from opening the doors on this level. Empty. All empty. A great big trap engineered to make a fool out of him and capture the one thing, the one person, he cared about.

When did that happen? How? When had intrigue and lust turned to affection? When did he start to care so much that the thought of Reba in Vivienne's grasp filled him with despair?

The old Gaston would shrug to know Vivienne held Reba captive. Such were the casualties of his vengeance. Except, for the first time in a long time, he did care. And her lion's pride cared. They all fucking cared, yet that didn't help them to find her, even though they went floor by floor searching for clues.

Even though they had their best techno geeks sifting for answers.

Nobody found a fucking thing.

He wasn't the only one to voice frustration.

Luna, the real Luna, put in another not-sopolite call to Melly. "I thought you fucking said you could access all the chopper companies in the area? How can you not know where they fucking went? Someone had to rent her that chopper."

"Unless she didn't rent," Melly snapped, her irritation emerging loud and clear, given Luna had her on speakerphone. "You wouldn't believe the assets this broad has. We keep finding more."

"You trying to tell me rich folk who own one don't have to register a flight plan or something?"

"Not at the height they fly."

"But she can't have gone super far. It's a helicopter. It's gotta land and fuel at some point."

"I'm looking for more addresses, but this heifer is clever. She hacked my hack. She's been toying with me, with us, the entire time. Every time I think I've unraveled her shit, another thread appears, and as soon as I pull on it, another snarly mess appears. The cow is everywhere."

The tendrils Vivienne had woven apparently stretched around the world. It was why Gaston never seemed able to fully eradicate her, why she constantly resurfaced, sometimes not for years at a time. As soon as she did, though, Gaston was there, poking at her. And for what? It wouldn't bring back his sister and now had cost him his lover.

"These delays are unacceptable. The longer it takes to find Reba, the more time Vivienne has to hurt her." Something he couldn't tolerate.

"Well, what the fuck would you like me to tell you?" Luna snarled. "I don't like it any better than you do, but unless you have some weird magic you can pull out of your ass, you're going to have to work with the process. Movies make it seem like big hacks and revelations happen overnight. These things take time."

Yet time was the one thing they didn't have.

What he did have was access to magic, special magic. But it would require a sacrifice. Blood magic always did. He should know, he was a necromancer and blood magic was his specialty. For those who didn't know, necromancy was the magic of the dead, but the dead mojo had to come from somewhere, and the strongest magic required he wield the killing blow.

He'd sworn to stop using that magic. Its dark seduction had pulled more than one necromancer to the dark side. Even now, the taint shadowed him. Made his need for vengeance pulse. *I told her I wasn't a good man.*

Yet, if he abstained and didn't use his power, then Reba might die.

The choice proved easy, the victim easier to wrangle than expected with Luna simply saying, "I can have what you need here in an hour."

Within two hours, bathed in fresh blood, Gaston knew where Reba was. In trouble, of course, but not just because of Vivienne. *What did you do, chaton?*

Chapter Eighteen

Hubba hubba.

Reba dreamed of him. Tony, her magical sugar. Striding toward her on a stormy landscape, his eyes flashing with gray fire, every inch of him big, lean, and mean, dressed in another one of his suits. How she wanted the proper amount of time and privacy to peel that off him and truly admire every inch of that superb body. *A body that is mine.*

And all mine.

Gimme.

"Where are you?" His words were everywhere, and nowhere. They caressed her with power, filled her with heat.

"I'm right here, sugar." She ran toward him and pounced when only a few feet away. A happy sound escaped her when he grabbed her mid-air and pulled her against him.

"Where is here? I need to see, *chaton.* Let me into you so I can see where you are."

"You are already a part of me," she purred, rubbing herself against him. "I marked you. You are mine. All mine."

"You did what?" For a moment, her big, bold Tony appeared taken aback.

"I marked you, in the stairwell. Remember that little love bite?"

"We'll talk of this later."

"Why not now?" she murmured, wrapping her arms around his neck and yanking him close. "We're all alone."

"Much as I'd like to, we have limited time, *chaton*. I am using magic to speak to you. I don't know where you are. Vivienne has stolen you. She thinks she can keep us apart."

"That heifer is really starting to piss me off."

"She's angered many of us, so let me in so I can find you."

"You want in, sugar? Then take me." She spread her arms wide. "Take me hard and fast."

"I think I shall." He lifted her off her feet, his big hands cupping her butt, holding her aloft, and even better, they were suddenly naked. Their skin rubbed, silky and electric. She wrapped herself around him, looking for as much contact as she could get. Her mouth melded to his, their kiss electric and never ending.

The tip of him pressed against her core, pressed and demanded entrance.

"Let me in." The words whispered against her.

"Yes." She gave her consent, the mark she'd given opening the way for him to penetrate her, not just with his dream cock but his essence. A part of him entered her, twined with her being, just like a piece of her had mixed with him during the bite.

The dual penetration shocked. Something heaved between them, a magic as old as life itself. For a moment, they hung, suspended in a perfect bliss, but all things eventually came down. However, something had changed.

Their souls now touched; she could feel it

inside. Each of them sharing a piece of the other that transcended simple bodily pleasure. *We are forever bound.* But that didn't mean he skipped the good part.

His dream self pounded into her, hard and fast, a vigorous claiming of her body that had her panting and keening his name until he came, shooting even more of himself inside her and jolting her with a bliss so intense she awoke with a heaving breath before crying his name, "Tony!"

Slap. The rude blow startled her, ripping her from pure bliss to...*where the fuck am I?* And with who?

Opening her eyes, she noted her second slap came from Vivienne, who stood beside Reba. Of more concern than the heifer's temerity in hitting was the fact that she found herself currently bound to an altar of stone.

Never a good thing. Especially since she was pretty sure a certain hero with a bullwhip had retired. No matter. She didn't need a man to save her. "I'll save myself," she muttered.

"Impossible. I know how to tie knots. And Gaston is not coming. I took you"—giggle—"and he has no idea you're here."

"And yet you're wearing lipstick, and is that perfume I smell?" Reba also noted Vivienne looked quite fetching with her blonde hair unbound and wearing a diaphanous white robe that delineated her nipples and the fact that someone didn't trim the rug down below. "Talk about showing off the goods," she mumbled. However, she found herself less concerned by Viv's whorish outfit than her situation. Not only did she appear to be attached to a stone altar, ankles and wrists fettered, she appeared to be wearing the same slutty gown as Viv. "What happened to my custom-made suit?" In the movies, they never stripped the superheroes. In the movies, the guy also saved the girl.

While usually a huge proponent of women's rights, in this instance, Reba would make an exception. It might be kind of hot to see Tony coming to her rescue.

Any time now.

"Now that you are awake, the ceremony can begin."

"What ceremony?"

"The one to change you, of course. I'd initially thought to make you into a whampyr. The female ones are so rare because they are so hard to make. But then it occurred to me that was a waste since you might still tempt Gaston after we're married."

"He's not marrying you."

"He will. He loves me. That's the reason why he's remained single so long. He's been waiting for this moment for a very long time."

"Exactly how old are you?" And what was Viv's secret?

"Twenty-nine, forever and more."

"You do realize, if you hurt me, that my pride will tear you to shreds."

"Your pride can't stop me. No one can. I've learned so many things. Things even Gaston couldn't imagine. I'm ready for him this time. This time I will prove I am worthy of his forgiveness, and I will have my prize."

A silver dagger lifted overhead as Viv held it aloft and chanted. It sounded like gobbledygook, with possible important bits. So Reba took a page from Meena's book and babbled.

"So, is it me, or is the shag below your belt a shade darker than on your head? Do you get it colored? I had an aunt that used to bleach her pubes blonde but kept her hair dark. Not sure why a person would do that. Just like I'm not sure about the whole pierced clit thing."

"Argh. Be quiet."

"No." Quiet was for people with nothing to say. Reba always had something to speak.

"You seem to think you're in control, and yet I hold the knife." Said blade dangled over Reba's chest.

"Then stab me and get it over with. Coward."

"I am not a coward."

"Then why tie me up?"

"Because people always flinch when I stab them." The feral smile almost deserved applause.

"Well, I believe in fair fights. And so should you." With a twist, Reba yanked the leg restraint free—people always did underestimate her strength—and kicked at Viv's arm. She connected hard and heard the clatter of metal as the dagger fell to the stone floor. But one limb free wouldn't do much. Reba strained, pulling on her beast side to snap the other fetters, simple fabric straps. A smart captor used silver chains.

And Reba had apparently forgotten Viv was smart. She stood at the door to the mausoleum with a nasty smile. "I guess this is where I mention that applying even ghoul magic on you seemed a waste. But feeding my pets? Make sure you aim your screams and agony at the camera. When I play the video later, I want Gaston to feel every ounce of this

185

moment."

Villain speech delivered, Viv exited, and the stone door to the crypt closed behind her with a heavy thump and then a click of a lock being engaged. More ominous than that was the grinding scrape of stone on stone.

A grinding that came from within the crypt, and her without a light to see. Personally, Reba thought it wasn't smoking that killed but the lack of a lighter at moments like these.

When in doubt, go feline. Except, when Reba went to pull on her inner kitty, it wasn't there. It snored in her mind, drugged and unresponsive.

Tony's ex-girlfriend is really starting to piss me off.

She couldn't count on her lion. No matter. Even from a young age, Reba's mother and father ensured she wasn't completely helpless. She dropped into a partial crouch, ready for anything, except the big gob of slimy goo that landed on her from overhead!

Suddenly, the hundreds of horror movies she'd seen over the years rushed back, and Reba did something very girly.

She screamed.

Chapter Nineteen

Why oh why did necromancers always have to be so cliché and battle in graveyards at night? It seemed in all the movies and shows it happened. Why did it also have to happen in real life?

Gaston exited his Lamborghini, the fastest car he owned to get to this massive cemetery outside of the city. And he meant massive. Thousands upon thousands lay buried here. So many bound souls, so many sparks underground and in the crypts dotting the landscape. Prisoners of their rotting flesh. Only fire, a fire that burned to ash, could release that energy.

Or a necromancer.

He still remembered the first time he touched a soulspark. His grandfather lay on his deathbed, and Gaston could see it so clearly, that strange mote of light trying to leave the body. So he helped it. His grandfather died, and then his father tried to have him killed. It was his grandmother who saved him, saved Gaston and his sister, teaching him the way of the dead.

A pity she'd forgotten to also show him how to live. With Reba, he planned to learn.

The sparks underground and in the vaults beckoned, but for the moment, he let the dead sleep. He turned in an almost full circle, his head lifted, much like a predator, scenting the wind, except he smelled on a different level, a more esoteric one. For him, the layers of arcane magic were colors overlaid on reality. Everything living, and everything dead, had a hue. But only one thing could outshine them all.

Without turning his head, he pivoted until he stood facing west and stalked through the graves. From behind, he could hear the rapid gunfire of wheels spitting gravel as more vehicles arrived behind him.

He paid them no mind. Just like he paid no mind to the dark pools hiding behind the statues. More of Vivienne's surprises. Let the city's alley cats and stray dogs take care of them. He had another task in mind.

Some of the monsters did not heed Gaston's grim countenance. On the contrary, they slunk out and thought to block his path.

"Do you really think you should get in my way?" he spoke aloud. "Tell your mistress she made a grave error."

The creatures did not listen, and the first of them, a thing with many tentacles, slithered over the tombstones and reached for him.

I don't have the time or patience for this. The obstacles in his path had to die, but he had to do it in a manner that wouldn't waste time. He knew of a most efficient way. He yanked the spark of life from the monsters, reached with ghostly fingers and snatched it from their bodies. They fell to the ground, disintegrating into ash, and the darkness in him reveled at his savagery.

He waved his hand, and the corpse dust blew from his path, and a new set of impediments took its place. Magical constructs never learned, so those that kept moving to block his path also died very abruptly—which caused a few complaints from his feline allies—*"Leave some for the rest of us, would you?"*

They would have to move faster then because he would allow nothing to stand in his way.

Not even Vivienne.

She stood before the mausoleum that held his shining goal. A past mistake that had haunted him for much too long.

It ends tonight.

"You're earlier than expected," she said, the torch she'd lit by the door of the crypt illuminating her pale hair and sheer gown. "Eager to reconnect, lover?" She plied him with a winsome smile.

It left him cold. "I am not your lover, and I'm not here for you. Move aside."

"Don't tell me you're pining for the feline. You're better than that. Better than her entire race. Breeding with the animals. It's disgusting."

"You are the only gross thing here. You are nothing but darkness." Indeed, nothing in Vivienne's aura held color. She was a void in the fabric, a hole that sucked in the energy around her.

Was that how he looked? How all necromancers looked? He'd never thought to ask, and most of his rare kind kept their auras locked tight.

"Why must you insist on condemning what we cannot change? We are creatures of the night."

"Stop stalling and move away from the door." The light beyond it beckoned.

And still Vivienne stood in his path. "You're already too late. By now, your whore has been torn apart by the residents of the crypt. They were asleep for so very long and are now so hungry."

"She's not dead." He would know. Just like Vivienne knew Reba still lived. It was why she stood in his way delaying.

"Move." He gave the order, not expecting it to work.

"No." Vivienne crossed her arms. "I do this for your own good. For our future tog—"

A wave of his hand and a pull on the magic in this place—so much magic in death—sent Vivienne soaring, far, but not so far that he didn't hear her hitting something. Good. He wasn't done with her yet.

He strode the remaining yards to the crypt and waved his hand to move the stone portal sealing. A lock on the door dared to get in his way. It crumbled at his crushing grip.

A heave on the door opened it, and through the torchlight that spilled past him, he noted a room full of gray bodies, ghouls, hunched and fierce, hands reaching for Reba. Slime coated every inch of her as she hung suspended from the ceiling, the candle sconces set in a chandelier on a short metal chain a precarious perch.

She waved and smiled. "Hey, sugar. Nice of you to come. Your ex and I were just getting to know each other. We hit it off so well she invited me to be dinner for her friends."

Crazy kitten. His kitten. "*Auudiaat.*" He hissed the word, and the ghouls in the room paused in their attempts to grab at Reba. As one, they turned to face him. They couldn't resist the command, but it would eventually fade. The undead required constant supervision to keep them in line.

"Come to me, and quickly. This won't hold them for long," he ordered.

Reba hopped down onto the altar then leaped over two standing bodies before hitting the floor with bent knees and racing to him. He braced himself for the pounce. She didn't disappoint.

Her legs wrapped around him. "Sugar, you're here."

"I told you I wouldn't let you come to harm."

"Aren't you just a perfect hero."

He winced. "Necromancers aren't heroes." Not in any stories.

"But I'll bet they get hot girls." She nipped his chin.

"I only need you," was the reply he uttered before he could think to hold it back.

"Isn't that touching." The sarcasm dripped, and Gaston turned slowly, very slowly, because intimidation was part of the game.

"I see you're back for more. Not a bright move, Vivienne. But I'm feeling benevolent tonight." Not really, but fighting Vivienne meant putting down Reba. Personally, he thought keeping her permanently attached to him had merit. "I'm going to give you a chance to walk away, and start over without me chasing you. I'm done getting revenge for my sister." Time to move on with his life—with Reba.

Only parts of his speech were acknowledged. Vivienne looked quite triumphant as she said, "I knew you'd forgive me. We are meant for one another."

"Never. Best forget me, Vivienne."

"You heard him, heifer. Tony is taken. As in mine."

Yes, hers.

"I don't speak to pets. Silence." Vivienne flung a hand outward, tossing magic Reba's way, and he deflected it.

"How dare you?" he snapped. "I gave you a chance, but you just won't listen. I'm done dealing with you. If you think I shall let you harm my soulmate—"

"What did you say?" Vivienne's features drained, and for a moment, she looked all of her many decades.

"I soul bonded with Reba. We are mated for eternity, and you know what that means. There will never be another woman for me."

"Seriously?" Reba blocked his view of Vivienne, her expression beaming. "That is like seriously hot. And I guess that means I'm not in trouble for marking you earlier. Which is kind of a bummer. I was looking forward to make-up sex later."

"How about we have didn't-die sex instead?" he muttered as the ground beneath them rumbled.

"That's not an earthquake, is it?" Reba asked, unwinding herself from his body.

"Ever see *Dawn of the Dead*?"

"Oh my God, it's the zombie apocalypse." Reba clapped her hands with evident glee. "You take me on the best dates."

"Remember, this isn't like the movies. Taking off their heads won't stop them. You have to sever limbs."

"Oh my God, we're going to fight the

undead." She sounded ridiculously excited. Which was why her pout made no sense. "And I don't even have my cool outfit anymore."

"Think again." He pulled it from a pocket and handed it to her before stepping away. He'd kept the scrap of material close, needing the object that touched her so intimately so that he could touch her mind while it slumbered.

The outfit she tried to unravel served to keep her out of the way for a moment as he confronted Vivienne. His former fiancée did not seem very pleased at the turn of events. Jealousy added decades to her features, and her lips twisted. Her arms stretched as she uttered a very guttural "*Surgere.*"

Play time.

A wind arose out of nowhere, chilly and carrying with it the scent of the grave. All around the graveyard the ground began to ripple as Vivienne reached out and stroked the sparks still within the decaying bodies. Stroked those energy motes and bound them to her will.

But she wasn't the only one who could do that.

Gaston lifted his arms to the sky and tilted his head back, his eyes closed. His lips parted as he whispered, "*Ego præcipio tibi.*" *I command thee.*

I am the master of the dead. Master of life and unlife. Bend to my will and fight.

Upon the dual demand from the necromancers, the dead rose to do battle.

Chapter Twenty

Color me fucking impressed. Even Reba's still drowsy feline admired what happened. Her mate could control the dead. Kind of freaky. More smelly than anticipated. And really fucking cool.

Tony even looked hot doing it, dressed all in black, a ghostly wind lifting his hair, his features stark and implacable.

"Damn." Luna's admiring remark as she sidled close made Reba smile.

"I know," she sighed happily. "He is so freaking hot. He's also mine. So eyes off him, biatch, or I'll tear them out of your face."

"I already have a man, so put your claws away."

"Are we standing back and letting his army of zombies do all the work, or can we play too?" Finger knuckles cracked as Joan, arriving from Reba's other side, stretched in preparation.

"It would be rude not to at least offer."

"The height of rudeness."

"And a waste of really good outfits," added Stacey, having joined the crew in a weaving and bouncing manner that saw her using gravestones and monuments to spring through the air and avoid the zombies already engaging in battle.

"We playing this one as cats?" Reba asked. Hers was still kind of yawning and in no shape to fight.

"Can't let the pussies out. Melly says someone tipped off the media. So there might be cameras, which means make it look good for the Internet and don't forget these." Luna handed out masks while Stacey gave Reba her handy-dandy bat. *Batter up.*

Hands slapped down as they chanted, "Baddest Biatches fight!"

With varying pitches of screams, the multi-colored superheroines sprang into action. Since they couldn't tell good zombies from bad, they just killed them all. Pulverized them into bone and grisly bits. Stomped and smashed until even those bits stopped moving. And a good time was had by all.

Taking a moment to breathe, Reba noted Gaston and Vivienne still faced off, their fight less physical, and yet, no one could doubt they battled. The strain showed on each face and posture.

Time to end this. Strutting across the battleground, Reba swung and connected with a partially decayed skull, caved it in, and moved on. Headshots only really blinded the zombies. It took serious work to completely obliterate them. But Reba had an idea about a shortcut.

I bet if I take out the zombie mistress, this fight will end. With that thought in mind, Reba stalked Viv, taking out the dead along her way. The plan would have worked, too, except Vivienne had something better than the dead watching her back. Something dropped out of the sky and scooped Reba up. Sharp talons dug into her shoulders, gripping her tight, tight enough that a flap of wings lifted Reba high above the ground.

Kind of cool except when the fucker got

several stories high, it let go and Reba plummeted. At times like these, Reba was quite convinced gravity hated her.

"Tony!" His was the name she gasped as the earth rose to say hello. Except she never hit the ground. A cold pillow of air cushioned her descent and she landed on her two feet. She immediately ducked.

A good thing because the winged monster came back for round two and narrowly missed her.

"Leave her alone." Tony held out a hand, and she could see the strain on his face as he tried to do something to the winged monster.

"While he's busy, time for a girly chat." Fingers tangled in Reba's hair as a minion grabbed hold and forced her to her knees before Vivienne.

She struggled, but the ghouls that had her weren't as easy to fight as the zombies. "Thank you for making this evening so exciting," Reba gushed as she twisted and managed to snap the wrist of the ghoul holding her. She evaded its other hand and dove at Viv, only to freeze when the witch spat, "*Duratus.*"

"I'm going to call cheating if you keep doing that," Reba grumbled.

"I tire of this game."

"Because I am winning."

"I have the upper hand. I'm in control," shrieked Viv.

It failed to impress Reba, who yawned.

"Impudent whore. Let's see how Gaston likes it when your blood soaks the ground."

The tip of the knife had only a moment to prick Reba's skin when the most primal roar shook the air.

"You. Will. Not. Hurt. Her. *Vaaaaade.*" He drew out the word, and while Reba didn't understand Latin, in that moment, tightly connected to Tony, she knew what it meant.

Begone.

And Tony added to the command a push, a hard push that saw zombies everywhere pausing; even the ghouls took note. Then shit started to explode. Like literally. Body parts spraying all over. The ghostly grip on her body loosened, allowing her to grab the knife aimed at her and rip it free. Something hit her in the back of the head, and she teetered. When she righted herself again, Vivienne was nowhere to be seen. All that remained? Gore and body parts, a veritable scene from a horror movie.

Cool.

Strong arms wrapped around her and lifted. Tony cradled her close. "And this is why you were supposed to stay at home," he grumbled against her, undaunted by the gore.

"But then I would have missed out on all the fun."

"Because a cemetery and hundreds of decomposing bodies is fun." He sighed. "Why must you be so perfect?"

"Hello, because I am a lioness. Now, before you tell me more about how awesome I am, did anyone see here Viv went? Is she dead?" Hard to tell with all the various body parts strewn all around.

"I don't know." He shook his head as he glanced around. "But I doubt we got so lucky. She's extricated herself from worse spots before."

"You mean she could come back?" Reba's

expression brightened as she shouted, "Hey, biatches, we might get a chance to do this again."

A cheer met her words, along with excited chatter. "Reba totally has the right idea with the bat, except mine is going to have spikes on it."

"It's called a mace."

"Not if it's long and skinny."

"Dumbasses, I'm going for a flame thrower. I say we shish-kebab their rotting butts."

And so on and so on. Even Melly, who taped the whole thing, had some advice to toss in, including plans to build a Taser for the undead.

A frown creased Gaston's brow. "Why was she videotaping this carnage? Surely she won't publish it."

"She'll have to if she wants to fuck with this investigation. How else to explain all these unburied bodies, which, again, I will add don't seem like they stink this much in the movies."

"Working with the dead is not pleasant for the olfactory inclined."

"A fancy way of saying it reeks. I'd prefer we stick to demons in the future. But I will say, working with you was a pleasure. You are some kind of badass." She draped her arms around his neck.

"How badass?"

"I'll show you how much if you get me into a shower." She leaned closer and whispered in her best naughty voice. "First I'm going to wash you, and then I'm going to make you a different kind of dirty."

"Your wish is my command."

"Not until the situation is under control, you disgusting lovebirds," Luna yelled. "Biatches. Do a graveyard sweep."

A sweep found some stragglers and another crypt full of ghouls. All dispatched, and before the first of the red and blue lights arrived, shifters by design, who helped stall for time while the cleanup crew arrived. They weren't the only team busy that night. The tech squad was dealing with the news crew that had seen part of the action. They'd be busy weaving a story to discredit the footage.

"Should we stay to help?" she asked.

"What are we? Servants?" Had to love a guy with that much arrogance.

Holy shit, I love the guy.

Even if he didn't have the power to teleport—a bit of a disappointment—he had brought the Lambo, and he also had access to a new condo, a big condo with a ginormous shower. Before she could get in, ghostly hands grabbed her and pinned her to a wall, a few inches off the floor.

"What are you doing?" she asked, very intrigued.

"It occurs to me, with all that's happened, I never showed you how I could pleasure you with no hands."

"I don't mind. I rather like your hands on my body."

"Me too, but it's harder to watch your face." He leaned a hip against the bathroom vanity, and his hooded eyes perused every inch of her body. "Seems to me you're wearing too many clothes."

Yes. Yes, I am. Good thing he planned to do something about it.

Invisible fingers peeled the bodysuit from her, tugging it over breasts with already hard tips, inching it over full hips, and far enough down her thighs that gravity finished the job.

The suit hit the floor, and she still hovered over it, the ghostly weight keeping her pinned. Her gaze was locked to Tony's; she loved how he watched her.

I should give him something to watch. "Should I touch myself for you?"

"No. I've got this." Her hands were yanked over her head, drawing her body taut, projecting her breasts. A push at her thighs parted them. She was at his complete and utter mercy. But it didn't frighten. On the contrary. It made her so very wet.

Tickling caresses started across her skin, almost like a chill wind that brushed and stroked over sensitized nipples, blew past her moist nether lips. The ghostly touches grew firmer, pinching the tips of her breasts, drawing a sharp gasp.

Her hips thrust forward as an invisible force stroked her sex.

"Tony." She moaned his name. He might not be the one caressing her with his flesh, but she never lost sight of the fact that he touched her. He watched her, watched as she undulated and moaned as he teased. He couldn't hide his excitement, his eyes glittering, his skin flushed. She could smell his arousal and wanted a taste.

Oops, she'd growled that aloud.

"Wouldn't you rather I finish pleasing you?" he asked, pushing away from the vanity, his fingers threading buttons through holes, revealing the skin of his chest.

"Touching and tasting you pleases me."

"But I wasn't done." His ghostly fingers penetrated her, deep and pushing against her sweet spot. She gasped, her channel clenching around…nothing.

"I need you, sugar. I want the real you, touching me. The real you, fucking me. And, yes, I am begging."

"Not until we wash the scent of death from our skin." He floated her into the shower and followed. The massive stall had numerous jets on both sides, and they shot forth water that started biting cold, drawing a yell that turned into a rumble of happiness as the water immediately warmed. He'd released his ghostly grip on her so she could raise her face into the spray and let it roll down her body, sluicing between her breasts.

Real hands, holding slippery, herb-scented soap skimmed over her skin.

"Is this better?" he asked.

She stole the bar of soap so she could stroke it over his flesh, hard muscles, toned ridges. She might have hummed in pleasure. "This is what I like. Hands-on, sugar. Hands"—she gripped his slippery cock—"on." She gave it a rub.

And then a tug. He felt so big in her hand, big and thick and so ready. However, she wanted to play. She'd earned a prize for her role today. Faster and faster she stroked him, and she could feel his cock pulsing in her hand, trembling on the edge.

Tony always tried so hard to be calm and in control, but with her, she knew how to get him to lose it.

He grumbled. "You're going to make me come if you don't stop."

Her reply. "Good."

Chapter Twenty-one

Good?

He was about to spew like an inexperienced boy, and she thought that was okay? Hell no. Time to remind her who dominated here. He spun her around until her hands were braced against the shower wall. He gripped her by the hips and leaned in close, his lips kissing her nape as he rubbed against her backside. "Not good, *chaton*. For once I want the whole experience. Not just rapid fumbles. Or quick pleasures. I want to savor your taste, feel you come on my tongue. And then, I want you to come on my cock."

"You say the hottest things. But that seems a little unfair. I want to have you in my mouth too. I haven't had a taste yet."

"I know how we can both get what we want. Do you trust me?"

"With my life."

A life that shone so brightly within her when they were together. She drew him like a beacon in the fog, so lively and bright she even dispersed the shadows on his soul.

A soft squeal left her as he manipulated her once more with power, flipping her upside down and hovering her at just the right height.

"If I fall, I'll kill you," she exclaimed.

"If you fall, I'd kill myself first. Never fear

with me. I will always keep you safe." And pleasured. He'd put her upside down for a reason. That reason involved her sliding her lips over his shaft, which drew a groan that rumbled past his lips and against her sex as he placed his mouth on her.

In his world, it was known as an aerial sixtynine, and it gave the most incredible maneuverability. He could hold on to her thighs, spread them wide, and lick her to his heart's content. While she, dear fucking gods he didn't believe in, she could suck. She inhaled him so hard he almost came, almost gave her what she wanted.

He might have lost his heart to her, but he wouldn't fail when it came to pleasing. His hips thrust in time to her mighty sucking while he savored the sweetness of her sex. He lapped between her lips, tasting her nectar, feeling the swollen arousal and slight tremors rocking her.

The distraction of her mouth around him proved distracting. As he licked her, she sucked him, a naughty 69 that brought him so close to release. Yet, this wasn't how he wanted things to end. He wanted to be inside her and for longer than a minute.

No quickie this time. It was one thing to claim it, another to manage it. She excited him too much.

Using his magic, he flipped her around, keeping her poised in the air, just above his cock.

"You're cheating," she exclaimed with no real heat, her eyes barely open, her passion keeping the lids heavy.

"I'm not the good guy, *chaton.*"

"Thank God, because bad is so much more fun." She reached for him, grabbing his cock and pulling it toward her. "Now fuck me. Fuck me hard."

How he loved it when she talked dirty. He loved even more doing dirty things to her. He grabbed her around the waist and pulled her hard against him, pushing the tip of his shaft past her slick lips, pushing into her tight and swollen sex. He savored every inch of heat and flesh pulsing around him.

Things started out slow. He wanted to savor it. She wanted none of that. She grabbed him and growled, "Give it to me."

He began to fuck her, slamming into her, harder and harder. Faster and faster, feeling her respond. Feeling her body tremble and quiver then tense as she screamed and came apart. And he came with her. Their tight bond meant he felt her pleasure as she felt his, and they were so mixed up that when one came the other did too, the force of it mighty. So mighty there were cracks in the tile when they were done.

He didn't care. He'd keep a tile guy on retainer for repairs if he had to because already he couldn't wait to take her again.

"That was pretty awesome," she said with a happy sigh. She clung to him tightly, her breathing heavy, her weight in his arms just right. "Will we break stuff every time we have sex?"

"Possibly."

"Cool. I always wanted to meet a man that could make the ground move. *Amabo te in perpetuum.*"

He went still. "What did you say?"

"*Amabo te in perpetuum.* I will love you forever. Isn't that what you told me in our dream?"

"You were actually there and never said anything this entire time?" It explained their close connection.

She grinned. "As if I'd make it that easy."

"I will love you forever. I waited a lifetime to find you. My perfect match. My soul mate."

And even death wouldn't part them. He'd make sure of that.

Epilogue

The Baddest Biatches became an overnight Internet sensation. The video of their seriously awesome zombie asskicking went utterly viral—people in awe of not just their fighting skills but the CGI and special effects. The lionesses were ecstatic.

Arik was livid. "How could you let them videotape?"

"It's not like they saw what we were or who we were." Indeed, just like a comic book, the use of a mask and a bodysuit blinded everyone to who they were. As a matter of fact, their masked identity made them only more desirable.

Although everyone got their names wrong. Reba's P became Perky. Luna's S turned into Sassy—which totally made her snarl. The other girls got nicknames too, some better than others. As for Gaston, his face was blurry, and he became known as the Sorcerer, the coolest name of them all, which also made Arik even more livid.

It seemed the pride alpha and the boys had gotten caught by the cops speeding on their way to the graveyard and spent a few hours downtown getting charged with reckless driving. That little favor cost the biatches, but it was well worth it not to share the fun with the guys.

And the fun didn't stop with the graveyard. It seemed Gaston lived a more interesting life than expected, or so Reba discovered when he took her back to Europe to visit one of his hidden estates. Someone had a title and a castle.

"You may call me your ladyship," she told her crew during a live video call from one of her four living rooms. Her biatches were so jealous.

The new role she played meant she had to upgrade her closet. Being the wife of a necromancer meant having outfits for every occasion.

"I'm a sorcerer, not a vampire," he remarked when he saw her dressed in her floor-length, form-fitting red gown with black lace trim.

"Is this your way of saying you don't like my dress?" She rubbed her hands over the fabric, skimming her curves.

"You do realize we're attending dinner with a few heads of state tonight?"

"Which is why I didn't wear panties. I figure we should have just enough time between the main course and dessert to slip away." She tossed Tony a coy smile with a hint of wicked.

"How did I ever live without you?"

Because of their connection, she heard the reply to his own question. *Before you, I didn't live at all. You are my life.* Just like he was her reason for pouncing.

Rawr.

*

"I need you deliver something safely." That was the only instruction the boss gave Jean Francois, other than telling him to wait on the airstrip.

And wait. If Jean were a less patient man, he

would have left, but the boss paid for his cell phone data, so he contented himself watching an episode of *Breaking Bad* on Netflix.

The sports car, a bright cherry red that surprisingly enough didn't come with a trail of screaming cop cars, screeched to a halt outside the plane. A curvy redhead in an outfit that should never see the light of day popped out of it, holding aloft a box.

At last. The package for delivery. About time.

"I'll take that." He held out a hand for it.

"Aren't you just a dollface. Thank you." She beamed as she handed it to him. His arms dropped at the weight.

"What the hell is in this thing? Rocks? A dead body?" One never knew with his boss.

"I can't tell you. It's a secret. All I can say is I need it."

"Need it for what?" he asked as she skipped toward the outside set of stairs leading up to the open door of the plane.

"We'll need it for our trip to the tropics."

We? "Our?"

"Didn't Gaston tell you? You're coming with me."

She was the package? "There must be a mistake."

"No mistake, sweetcheeks. Once you store that box on board, don't forget to grab my luggage in the trunk."

"I think there's been a mistake. No one said anything about a trip." Surely Gaston didn't hate him that much. He'd bet this was the work of his boss's new girlfriend. Sending him away with her pet cat. *Do*

I look like a pet sitter?

The feline in question didn't seem to notice his reluctance. She paused in the doorway of the plane, one foot still on the top step, a vibrant sight that drew his eye—and a red pinprick of light from a laser sight.

Bang.

The End?

Not quite because we'll be seeing more of Stacey in
When A Lioness Growls.

See EveLanglais.com for more books and information.

CPSIA information can be obtained
at www.ICGtesting.com
Printed in the USA
LVOW12s2146080317
526607LV00003B/229/P